Mesdames of Mayhem

13 CLAWS

Editor: Donna Carrick
Copy editor: Ed Piwowarczyk

CARRICK
PUBLISHING

13 Claws

An anthology of crime stories

by the Mesdames of Mayhem

Copyright Mesdames of Mayhem 2017
Copyright Carrick Publishing 2017

Edited by Donna Carrick

Copy edited by Ed Piwowarczyk

Formatting by Donna Carrick

Cover Art by Sara Carrick

Carrick Publishing

Print Edition 2017
ISBN 13: 978-1-77242-069-2

"A great mix of shuddery dark and tongue-in-cheek funny. What devious minds all these nice women have. (Murdog liked the stories as well.)"

~ *Maureen Jennings, author of Murdoch Mysteries, the Tom Tyler series and Christine Morris Books.*

Contents:

Foreword

By Donna Carrick

The Mesdames of Mayhem are an eclectic group of crime writers who approach the art of storytelling from many angles.

Through years of working together, we've discovered that we share a number of common passions.

First, there is our enthusiasm for the crime genre—writing, reading and discussing our work.

Second, and of equal importance, is our love of animals.

Most of us have enjoyed the companionship of a beloved pet, or two, or more…. As friends and colleagues in the crime genre industry, we've had many opportunities to share our experiences of the fur-or-feather variety.

When my family lost our golden retriever, Daisy, in October of 2016, it was the Mesdames of Mayhem who rushed forward with heartfelt condolences. It was the Mesdames (and Monsieur) who understood our grief and our cherished memories.

On behalf of the Mesdames and Monsieur of Mayhem, I'd like to dedicate this anthology to every pet who has ever blessed us with love.

Daisy, you are forever in our hearts.

Donna Carrick
Carrick Publishing

MESDAMES OF MAYHEM

DOG TRAP

By Melodie Campbell

It wasn't her.

Rick knew it now, scrolling through email messages, stopping on the last one. The words were there, purportedly from her, but written by someone else. Now he was certain. The trap had been set, and he had proof.

He slumped back in the worn gray swivel chair to think. And mourn. On the floor beside him, the small golden retriever puppy whimpered in sympathy.

More than a week ago, suspicion had set in. How could he explain it? A different use of words…not something you could explain to anyone else. But somehow, it seemed forced. *It wasn't right.*

He and Tess had been close for months. You got to know someone pretty well writing every day online. It had started innocently enough, in a discussion group about dogs. Before he knew it, they were talking privately by email, about everything under the sun.

Even though they were only words on a screen, he found himself depending on them for company and sympathy. Someone to share your his thoughts with. It cut through the loneliness of everyday living. Before long, he was living from night to night, rushing through each teaching day, eager to get home to his computer to see what message she had left for him.

Soon he was obsessed.

Almost immediately, he began to fantasize about her. She would be dark-haired, he knew. Somehow he couldn't visualize a blonde Tess. It didn't fit the sultry image he had built in his mind.

She would have a woman's body, soft and sensuous. Not like the rail-thin college girls who shared his daylight hours.

Tess shared his nights.

It was astounding how much he knew about her without even having seen her. He knew, for example, that *Carmen* was her favorite opera. Indeed, that was the way he pictured her: black hair, full red lips, head thrown back in endless laughter at the world.

She hadn't tried to hide her identity. Rick knew her full name, and where she worked. He also knew she was married and unhappy. He had even dreamed about rescuing her—a silly, juvenile thought at his age. That was the problem, of course—Rick's age. It was so easy to be someone else when hiding behind a computer screen. What harm could it do to fib a little, and pretend to be 45, instead of 54? A careless switch of digits, if he ever needed to explain it.

Now he was cursing himself. He should have been honest. Then he could have suggested they meet for coffee. Why had he been such a coward?

Rick swung back to the monitor and stared at the last damning message. Why would anyone pretend to be her? At first, he'd been angry. Now, he was terrified. This was more than a joke. The imposter knew her very well...her work life and her personal details. Tess hadn't spoken of going away, and Rick knew darn well she would have mentioned it in a message. So who was covering up her sudden absence? And more important—where was she now?

Sitting at the keyboard, Rick felt alone like never before. Gravely certain, he forged a course of action. One

4

hand reached for the printer. The other hand picked up his cell phone.

***

On Friday morning, two police officers stood at his door.

"Strangled," the taller officer said. "Neatly and quickly. She didn't suffer much. We thought you'd want to know."

Rick nodded and gestured them in. He watched with dull eyes as the two officers crossed to the other side of the kitchen table. Carefully, he reached for the chair behind him and tried to compose himself.

"The husband?" he asked quietly.

"Abusive bastard." The tall officer scowled. "But thanks to your phone call, we got him. Denied it at first, then cried like a baby. Buried her in the garden. Covered the whole plot with flowers. We caught him tending it." He shook his head in disbelief.

The second officer shifted his ample weight on the small kitchen chair. "Answer me something," he said. "I can understand how you might be suspicious, writing each other every day. But how did you know for sure that an imposter had taken over?"

Rick's mouth twisted. He reached down to pat the head of the puppy at his feet. "Imagine living with someone for weeks and months. And then suddenly, you realize she looks the same, but she's an imposter. You know it the second the lights are out."

He looked off into the distance, as the dog lazily licked his hand.

"It can be like that on a computer screen…like living with someone's mind. Knowing their intimate thoughts, their dreams, the essence of them."

Rick sighed. He felt old—older than he had in months.

"I was suspicious at once," he said. "So I set a trap. One that the real Tess would never fall for."

The two officers leaned forward. Richard pulled a folded sheet of paper from his shirt pocket and explained, "Here's the last message I got."

Subject: First day at school

Message from Rick:
Alex's first day at school was a disaster! She hid behind me the whole time.

Message from Tess:
Don't worry, Rick. A lot of children have a hard time on their first day. I remember crying for hours when I was five.

Rick carefully refolded the paper into squares and handed it to the baffled officer. Then he gazed down at the contented puppy, giving it one more pat.

"I don't have any children," he said simply. "Alex is my dog."

About Melodie Campbell

Melodie Campbell has been called Canada's "Queen of Comedy" by *The Toronto Sun*. Library Journal compared her to Janet Evanovich.

Melodie has won the Derringer, the Arthur Ellis, and eight more awards for fiction. In 2015, she made the Amazon Top 50 bestseller list, sandwiched between Tom Clancy and Nora Roberts. Also that year, she was a finalist for the Arthur, along with Margaret Atwood. (Atwood won.) Melodie is the past Executive Director of Crime Writers of Canada. She has been on faculty at Sheridan College since 1992. *The Bootlegger's Goddaughter* is her 11th novel.

Website: www.melodiecampbell.com
Twitter: @MelodieCampbell
Facebook: MelodieCampbellAuthor

HOMEBODIES

By Rosemary McCracken

A gentle pressure on my eyelids roused me from my afternoon nap. I opened one eye to see Romeo standing on his hind legs, a paw raised, peering intently at my face.

"Damn cat!" I hoisted myself into a sitting position on the sofa. "Get down!"

Satisfied that I was still in working order, Romeo sauntered out of the room, his tail waving like a plume.

"He was worried about you, Henry," Ellie said when I told her about it over dinner.

"Worried where his next meal would come from," I grumbled. "I'm the one who feeds that damn cat."

***

I have never liked cats—I've always thought they knew too much—so I looked with dismay at the marmalade tabby that Ellie had brought home from the animal shelter.

"You've been talking about traveling," I said as I watched him explore the main floor of the house. "We can't go far with a cat." We had both retired the year before, and Ellie wanted to see the world.

She tossed her head, setting her strawberry blond curls dancing. "Cats are very self-sufficient," she said. "One of the neighbors will come in and feed him."

"This cat is not a good idea."

"Nonsense, Henry. You think you don't like cats, but you'll come to love this one. I promise."

Ellie always got her way. She'd got her way ever since we'd married 35 years before, and I had no idea how to change tack at this point.

She'd spent three decades teaching high school English, so when the cat discovered the Juliet balcony off our main-floor family room, she named him Romeo. But she soon admitted that was a misnomer. Not only had this cat been fixed, but he was a house cat. Other than demanding to be let out on the balcony now and then, he showed no inclination to go outdoors. "Should've called him Henry after you," she said, patting my paunch. "Henry I and Henry II, my two homebodies."

But he answered to Romeo, so the name stuck.

At first, he didn't know what to do about stairs. "He must've lived in an apartment before he was sent to the shelter," Ellie said, as we watched him hesitate at the top of the staircase to the basement. "Take him down, Henry. Show him his bed and his litter box."

I gingerly put a hand under him. He squirmed, stepped aside and whipped a paw full of claws across my arm.

Ellie picked him up. I followed them downstairs, holding a towel around my bleeding arm. She placed the cat in the litter box she'd set up in the laundry room. He hopped out of it, ignored the new cat basket she'd bought for him, and headed into the furnace room next door. He settled himself on an old rug that was spread over two boxes, folding his front paws into his chest and regarding us with sphinx-like eyes.

"He's telling us that this will be his quarters," I said.

Ellie heaved a sigh. "If that's what he wants." She moved the litter box and the cat basket into the furnace room.

"The furnace room is a good place for him," I said as we went upstairs. "It has a door we can close at night."

Ellie looked alarmed. "We don't want to lock him in like a prisoner."

"Just at night. We'll put him in there before we go to bed."

I didn't want him wandering around my home while I was asleep.

***

After that scratch, I did my best to keep out of Romeo's way. But Ellie volunteered at the animal shelter three afternoons a week and spent another three afternoons at the art gallery, so I became his go-to guy for dinner. At five on the dot, he proclaimed with a raspy yowl that it was time for food, and hurled himself against my legs until I did something about it.

I found myself on breakfast duty as well. After years of rising at six every morning to teach high school, I couldn't sleep any later. Romeo called from the basement as soon as he heard me on the main floor. When I opened the door to his quarters, he raced up to the kitchen letting the world know that he was starving.

I never tried to pick him up again, but he kept close tabs on me. While I worked on my historical novel, he'd watch from the armchair in my study, and follow me whenever I took a break. And he took over my armchair in the family room, making it very clear that it was his. I had to settle for a corner of the sofa.

Ellie fussed over him, brushing his coat and feeding him gourmet cat treats. She tried to get him to curl up on her lap when we watched television in the evening. He tolerated the grooming and accepted the treats, but he refused to get on her lap. He kept his distance on the armchair.

"He's more your cat than mine," she complained one evening when Romeo had refused her lap again.

"Nonsense. He doesn't get on my lap, and I wouldn't want him to. Besides," I added with a sideways glance at her, "didn't I hear you say that cats don't belong to anyone? They're our masters."

As soon as she went to bed after the evening news, Romeo would leave the armchair, and stretch out on the carpet in front of the TV while I watched late-night sports highlights. From time to time, he'd turn his head to see what I was up to.

After sports highlights, I'd read for a while. Romeo was usually asleep when it was time for me to turn in. I'd call his name, and he'd get up and follow me to his quarters downstairs.

***

Being under Romeo's surveillance put me increasingly on edge. I needed a change of scene, so that fall I started tutoring at the public library. Two afternoons a week, I met with a group of high school students, and tried to bring Canadian history to life for them.

"About time you got out of the house," Ellie said when I told her about the tutorials. "You've gained a good 10 pounds since you retired. It's not healthy."

The morning of my first tutorial, she issued a couple of orders. "Get a haircut," she said. "Long white hair is not attractive. Unless you tie it back."

She knew I'd sooner put on a skirt and high heels than wear my hair in a ridiculous mantail like her friends at the art gallery.

"And drop into the travel agency. Pick up some brochures," she added. "I've never been to Europe, and its art galleries are on my bucket list. I want to see the Mona Lisa and the statue of David."

"Why go to Europe? We've got your uncle Jeremy's paintings right here in the family room."

"We've been looking at those two paintings since Jeremy died 18 years ago. I realize that J.R. Robitaille and Sean Larmer were great Canadian artists, but there's a whole world of art to see. Not to mention famous places: the Ponte Vecchio, Pompeii, the Acropolis, Blarney Castle. We're retired now, and it's our chance to see them."

I'd already seen a lot of the world. When I finished university, I made a grand tour of Britain and Europe. Fifteen countries in 21 days. And now I could visit any place I chose on my computer without jet lag, pickpockets and strange food. My home was my castle. That was something Romeo and I had in common. The problem was we called the same castle home.

***

Ellie didn't comment on my cropped hair or ask about travel brochures—which I'd forgotten—when I returned home around six. She was sitting at the kitchen table, nursing her hand. "Romeo was in a terrible state when I got in," she said. "Howling as though he hadn't been fed for a week. When I put his bowl on the floor, he nicked my hand."

She held it up. It had a red scratch on it.

"Put some Polysporin on that." I told her. "What time did you get home?"

"Five-thirty, as usual."

"He likes to eat at five."

Romeo ambled into the kitchen, and threw me a dirty look. I knew I'd better stay clear of his claws.

***

The three of us settled into an uneasy routine. Romeo put up with Ellie serving him a late dinner twice a week. She wore oven mitts when she set his bowl on the floor.

She brought home dozens of travel brochures, and spread them over the dining room table. When the table was covered, she put brochures on the dining room chairs. She thrust brochures under my nose while I was watching television. I put a pillow over my head when she talked about Florence in the middle of the night.

Romeo continued to follow me around the house. The bathrooms were the only places I could get away from him. And our bedroom, when he was down in his quarters for the night.

***

I woke up when something landed on my chest. I touched a warm ball of fur, then reached for the switch on the lamp cord. It was 3:15 a.m., and Romeo was looking down at me. He patted my cheek with a paw.

"How did you get up here?" I asked him.

He jumped off the bed and stood in the doorway.

"What is it?" Ellie asked beside me.

Romeo gave a soft meow. He walked to the top of the staircase, then back to the bed.

"Romeo's here," I said. "He's trying to tell us something."

"How did he get out of his quarters?"

I heard a noise downstairs, and turned to Ellie with a finger over my lips. "Stay here," I whispered and switched off the lamp.

I followed Romeo downstairs, avoiding the step that creaked. The farther down we went, the chillier the house became. A light in the family room and the streetlights outside bathed the ground floor in a grey gloom.

From the dining room, I could see a man dressed in black moving around the family room. He had taken the J.R. Robitaille off the wall and was holding it by its frame. The door to the Juliet balcony stood open.

Romeo jumped on a chair and looked up at me. He seemed to think I'd know what to do.

The thief had his back to me, and I charged into the family room. He turned around, dropping the painting. He grabbed my arm and threw me onto the floor, but I took him down with me. He shook me off, sprang up and picked up a knife on a bookcase shelf. As I backed away on the floor, Romeo leaped onto the chair beside him and raked a paw across the hand that held the knife. The man howled, dropped the knife, and clutched his hand.

I grabbed the knife.

Ellie ran into the room in her dressing gown, brandishing our giant wooden pepper mill. She swung it at the thief's head like a baseball bat. He slumped to the floor.

"Steve Vernon!" she cried, looking down at him.

"You know him?" I asked.

"From the art gallery."

"Should have known from the hair." His long brown hair was tied back in a mantail.

I bound his hands together with duct tape. By the time the police arrived, he'd regained consciousness.

***

"A cat?" the police officer asked.

"Yes, a cat by the name of Romeo," Ellie said. "He scratched the thief. Made him drop the knife."

I held the knife out to the officer.

He shrugged and opened a plastic bag. I dropped the knife into it.

"Everyone's pet is special," he said, and turned to his partner. "I can see the headline in the *Sun* tomorrow: Cat Nabs Cat Burglar."

Romeo kept out of the way while the officers were in the house. As soon as they'd taken the thief away, he headed straight for the bowl I'd filled for him.

I joined Ellie on the sofa in the family room. "Steve Vernon works at the art gallery," I said.

"He's a graduate student doing a three-month internship." She examined her manicure. "He was in the staff room when I was bragging about our paintings the other day."

She looked up at me. "Stupid of me, I know."

There was nothing I could say to that, so I took her hand. "I wonder how Romeo got out of the furnace room."

"Maybe you didn't close the door properly," she said.

"I'll take a look."

She followed me downstairs.

The door to the furnace room was closed. "Supercat!" Ellie cried.

I looked behind the clothes dryer where there was about six inches of space between the machine and the wall. I had punched out a hole in the drywall just above the floor for the hose that connects the dryer to an outside vent in the furnace room wall. I couldn't install a vent in the laundry room because the walls were covered with cupboards and shelves.

The hose was no longer attached to the machine.

"He crawled through the hole in the wall," Ellie said beside me.

I nodded. "Must've pulled off the hose when he heard something upstairs."

"He thought you were up early."

"No, he knew it was too early for me to be up."

Ellie announced that she was exhausted when we returned to the main floor. "But we can't go back to bed," she said. "We're giving our statements at the police station at nine. Shall we have a cup of tea?"

I put on the kettle while she settled herself on the sofa. When the tea was brewed, I brought a cup over to her. Romeo walked into the room as I sat down with mine.

"Come sit with us, Romeo," Ellie crooned, patting a spot on the sofa. "Here, sweet puss."

He jumped into his armchair, and made himself comfortable.

"Let him be," I said. "He knows where we all belong."

About Rosemary McCracken

Rosemary McCracken writes the Pat Tierney mysteries. *Safe Harbor*, the first novel in the series, was a finalist for the British Crime Writers' Association Debut Dagger. It was published by Imajin Books in 2012, followed by *Black Water* in 2013 and *Raven Lake* in 2016.

"The Sweetheart Scamster," a Pat Tierney story in the anthology, *Thirteen*, was a Short Mystery Fiction Society Derringer Award finalist in 2014. Jack Batten, the *Toronto Star's* crime fiction reviewer, calls Pat "a hugely attractive sleuth figure."

Rosemary has worked at newspapers across Canada as a reporter, arts writer and reviewer, and editor. She now lives in Toronto and teaches novel writing at George Brown College.

Visit Rosemary at her website:
http://www.rosemarymccracken.com/
Her blog site: rosemarymccracken.wordpress.com/
On Facebook
or Tweet with @RCMcCracken:

THE OUTLIER

By Catherine Astolfo

If I'd paid attention to Marvin, none o' this would've happened. For that matter, I should've seen the signs left by the burglar when he cased the joint.

Whenever I take my semi-annual trips to St. John's, stocking up for the seasons, the hours of hard driving there and back again take their toll on the old man I have become. Especially the early winter drive.

This little spot isn't called Back Side Harbor for nothing. We're the ass end of a narrow strip of land— technically an isthmus—that juts out into the Atlantic.

Back Side is an outport. Pay attention to that word *out*. It has a lot of uses here in Newfoundland. Outport family names go back many decades, even though most o' those families moved out of here during resettlement. There are a dozen villagers left, give or take. They think their shit smells good because they have those historical names. However, since none of us goes out, it's hard to tell who's still here and whether they really are a Gill or a Butt.

I'm an outlier, a person who's come from away, so I get even less attention from any of the harbor dwellers. Which suits me just fine, since being out of contact is my goal.

I live on the hill above the harbor in a little cottage. Been here 10 years now. One big room, with a living area and a kitchen, runs along the front part. The back has a bedroom and a bathroom.

I have a corn-fed stove that keeps the whole place warm in winter and the windows send cool ocean breezes in the summer. No electricity, but a big old generator gives me all the power I need.

With such a small space to look after, you'd think I'd've taken note that first day when I found my mattress shifted slightly on the bed. Next, the shutter in the kitchen left open. The third day, a lack of snow on the doorstep, as though it had been blown away by someone's boot.

My excuse—I was just so damn tired. That trip to the city is brutal. I'm creeping onto 90 years old next year, if I'm still here. I can't do three whole days away from home any more. I don't sleep well in those cheap hotels. Everything is just so…noisy. Like a big loud cell block in a federal prison.

The day the kid arrived, I was still tired from the trip. Not to mention the tasks I'd had to face when I got home.

I drowsed all afternoon with Miss Kitty. She's a big old tabby cat who wandered by one day and stayed. She likes to curl up on my stomach, makin' biscuits in the blanket with her paws.

I sat and listened to the CBC on the radio. Played some solitaire. Did nothing and paid no attention, just like Miss Kitty.

Marvin, on the other hand, sniffed and snorted everywhere during those four days. He knew there was something off. He can always tell when a stranger invades our privacy.

Here's the quick version of Marvin's story.

I was comin' back from one of those voyages to the city when we were stopped on the highway by a rollover.

From out of the damaged back end of the truck, down the road trotted a whole bunch of pigs. They'd been hauling them off to the bacon factory.

Only Marvin made it as far as my car. The rest of the porcine escapees got recaptured, run over by traffic on the other side, or disappeared into the brush. I watched this big guy waddle along the side of the highway, head up, going who knew where. He was simply scramblin' fast as he could in the opposite direction of that truck.

Thing is, I didn't think about what I did. I certainly didn't expect the result I got, either. I admired that pig's determination to get away so I leaned over and opened my passenger door. And into the old car hopped Marvin.

As it turns out, pigs make great pets. They're clean, smart, they'll eat whatever's on offer, and they like people. Marvin's a bit stubborn, likes his own way in things, but so do I and so does Miss Kitty. We make a great trio.

The kid came at night, when I was fast asleep. There were three signs of his invasion that I could not miss.

First, the sound of a chair falling over (though I didn't know that was what caused the bang until later).

Second, Miss Kitty used her claws in fright to lift herself off me, even digging below the blanket and through my long johns.

Third, Marvin made his squealing noise, a throaty, screechy kind of sound that feels like pins in your ears.

I sat straight up in my bed and, what with the noise and the cat's nails, soon had my feet on the ground.

I didn't need to tiptoe to the front of the house. Marvin was raising such a racket that a truck could've driven through the living room and no one would have heard it.

The young guy was sprawled out on the floor. He'd obviously come in through the kitchen window, stepped on that rickety chair and sent it and himself tumbling to the floor. Unfortunately for him and Marvin, he landed on the pig.

I went for the guy without a second thought. Lifted him off my pet. Flipped him over onto his stomach. Pulled his left arm behind and upwards till he made squeals of his own.

In the meantime, Marvin scrambled to his feet, still carrying on, but now he was snorting with indignation.

I reached over to the drawer nearby and got my fingers on a couple of cable ties. I soon had the asshole's hands tied behind his back.

I rolled him over and clipped his ankles together for good measure. Then I lit the kerosene lamp.

I checked on poor Marvin, who was still mad, but he looked and felt okay.

Then I had a long gander at my intruder.

He was a young 'un. Early 20s, maybe even late teens. Fair hair and freckles. At the moment, his baby blues were liquid with fear and shock.

I figured he didn't expect me to be home. Even if he thought I might be here, he didn't think an old guy like me could take him down.

I put the chair back on its feet and sat.

"So, b'y, what the feck're ya doin' in my house?" I asked, using as good a Newfoundland accent as I could manage.

He didn't struggle. Just lay there panting for a moment.

"Are you gonna call the cops?" he finally gasped.

"Not much point to that. They're all the way over to Fishy Cove, and they're closed at night."

I waited a moment.

"That's all you got to say?"

The boy's eyes were clearing. He almost looked defiant.

"I knew you'd say that."

"Say what?"

"About not callin' the cops."

"Did ya now?"

I got up and stretched, feeling the takedown in my lower back and shoulders.

"Since we're all up, we might as well have a cuppa tea and a yarn. What do you t'ink?"

My visitor had the grace not to answer.

We needed something to cheer us up. After all, we'd suffered a big shock.

I gave Marvin one of his favorite treats, a mishmash of broccoli, carrots and squash. He snorted a few times, but soon got distracted by the food.

Miss Kitty still hadn't surfaced, but I put some tuna down in a bowl just in case.

I lit the gas stove and put the kettle on the burner. I got the Baileys from the icebox and poured a good measure into my teacup.

While the water boiled I took my handcuffs down and swiftly replaced the cable ties. I let him keep one hand free while the other dangled from the chain and eyehook on the wall.

He yanked on the chain once but seemed satisfied that he was stuck. He settled in.

I pulled my old armchair closer to the wall and propped the kid against it so he could sit up.

Once the tea was ready, I sat on a chair, angled so I could see the young man's face. We sipped in silence for a few minutes. Like he'd just dropped in for a nice winter's chat.

He should've thought to dress like a mummer, hide his face under a mask. Either the guy was dumb, or he was new to breaking and entering.

"You thought I wouldn't be home, wha?"

"No, I thought I could sneak in."

That made me laugh.

"Well, I'd say the arse fell out of 'er on that one. You from around here?"

He shook his head. "I'm from Vancouver."

"Whoa. You're way off your patch, aren't ya?"

"So are you."

I chuckled and shook my head.

"Mind now, you're the one come into my house. I gets to ask the questions."

"I know who you are."

"It's my turn, then. Who owns ya? Related to an outport family?"

"You're not a Newfie. Stop talking like one."

I laughed heartily.

"Reminds me of that old joke. The mother says to her wayward boy, 'Son, why-a you do deese t'ings to-a me?' and the son says, 'Ma, why are you talking like that? We're not Italian.'"

I guffawed some more. I was beginning to have fun. That's what comes from living without other humans. You are easily amused when they do show up.

I leaned over, still laughing. When I slapped him across the face, he looked as though I'd betrayed him.

"What. Are. You. Doing. In. My. Home." I punctuated each word so he could understand me above the likely ringing in his ears.

Tears slid down his cheeks, but he was still determined to be rude and a liar.

"I needed money."

I waved my hands around the cottage.

"And you thought I'd have lots of it hidden here on the hill above Back Side Harbor. You are dumber than I thought and that's pretty dumb."

"I meant…I thought I could take something and sell it."

I smiled at him. He really was stupid.

"Like my teacup?" I held it aloft, displaying the side with a prominent chip. "How much will this beauty fetch? Was ya born on a raff?"

When I stopped laughing, I scowled and leaned over him, snatched his empty cup.

"Maybe you can tell the truth about the *who*. Who are you? No ballyraggin' this time."

I used the quiet, menacing voice that tends to encourage reluctant truth telling.

He pulled the lids over his big eyes, fear crowding out the defiance. He thought he could hide the sudden vulnerability he was feeling.

"No…what?"

Why are there so many stupid criminals these days? In my day, it took cunning and careful study of the details. The what-ifs, the contingencies, the back stories.

"Don't feckin' lie to me, b'y." This time I must admit my voice rose a little.

"I…my name is Brent Hillyard. I do come from Vancouver. That's the truth."

"Well, Brent, nice to meet ya. I'm Jason."

"No, you're not."

"Jaysus, idd'n you a stunned one?"

He cried out when the cup landed on his forehead. Bled like a sucker, too.

I got another cup out of the cupboard and fixed us more tea. Mine got an even larger dollop of Baileys than last time.

I pulled out the lassy buns I'd bought in St. John's. A rare luxury that the stupid kid in front of me, had he any manners, ought to appreciate. I was a regular Martha Stewart.

I handed him a clean handkerchief, too, so he wouldn't get blood on my floor. It's a bitch to get that stuff out of the carpet.

I munched on one of those delicious treats while he blotted at his cut. With any kinda luck, he wouldn't feel like eating.

"Lots of people calls me Jason," I said between bites. "That's what you'll call me, too."

He said nothing. Sulking, I supposed.

"So. We gots the *who* and the *why*. I needs to know the *how*. Or did I get the why? I've been t'inkin'. Maybe there's another reason you tripped all this way to the Back Side. You thought I might have some souvenirs. Any other reason?"

He looked pretty scared now. Sometimes people get that way when they've been hurt. Not too many of us is used to being doused on the head. Or on any other body part, for that matter.

"I…I'm kind of a reporter."

"Kind of? Either you are or you aren't. You can't be kind of. That's like you're kind of a moose or not."

He considered that for a moment. "I work in the mailroom right now. My dad's the chief editor, and he insisted I start at the bottom."

"Uh-huh. Now that's some wise, b'y."

"I thought if I uncovered a big story, he'd…well, he'd promote me faster."

"I dies at dat, fella. You are some full o' yourself. So you takes off work and comes all the way out 'ere cuz you t'ink I'm a big story. Huh."

I took another lassy bun.

"I ought to be flattered, I suppose. After all these years, I'm still a big story."

"You'll always be a big story," he said. "No one will ever forget what you did."

I stood up so quickly that my chair fell backwards.

"I'm havin' trouble believing a dimwit like you found me when no one else has. Maybe you should use those smarts to show your father you're a hard worker instead of trying to take the easy way around."

I stretched up and back, hands on my hips. Took a few deep breaths, in my nose and out my mouth. Ten years of perfect solitude, no fools to hound me, no idiots to spread vicious rumors of my supposed exploits.

And this goof, this lowlife idiot, had cracked the mystery of my whereabouts? I had a difficult time calming down, I tell you.

"You might as well tell me how, lad."

I righted my chair and sat down again, folded my arms and tried to achieve a kindly old man's expression.

"Have a lassy bun first. You must be 'ungry."

While he munched, he stared at me the whole time. I was a museum piece to him. I gazed right back, knowing full well the emotions I felt weren't visible.

The boy's expression, on the other hand, clearly displayed curiosity, horror, fear, and even a hint of defiance.

The newspapers always described my eyes as *dead*. How can eyes be dead in the face of a person who is alive? Impossible. They meant devoid of feeling. Uncaring, calm, nothing to see here. Back away. That's what they should have said.

This boy didn't back away, though. I wondered if, instead of stupid, he was a bit like me. He cared about nothing and no one. In his case, his sole purpose was self-aggrandizement. Maybe he was more worthy than I thought.

"All right. Hope you liked your breakfast."

He nodded, unable to halt the manners he'd clearly been taught.

"Yes, thank you."

I let the Newfoundland accent slip, winding him up, letting him think he'd gotten through.

"Tell me how you found me, and maybe I'll give you a story to take away with you."

Brent sat up straighter. He was clearly pleased and excited.

He would never make it as a reporter. He was far too easily manipulated.

"I have some connections in the prison. The last one you were in," he said.

I nodded, though I felt like saying, "Well, duh."

"My friend was a guard there. He got me an interview with your old cellmate."

"*Brent.* You broke into my home. I am hosting you with great patience. I don't expect lies."

"Oh yeah, yeah, sorry, I meant a guy who was in the same segregation block as you. You know, the protective solitary cells where…"

"I guess I know all that. Stay on point."

He nodded, eager to please me now.

"Yes, yes, of course. Anyway, this prisoner talked quite a lot to my friend. He claimed he'd heard you say to your lawyer that if they ever granted parole, you'd go to the other side of the country, like Newfoundland, and hide out."

Those damn cells were like echo chambers.

"Okay. So did you search all over Newfoundland for the last 10 years and just get lucky?"

"Of course not. I was just nine when—"

All I had to do this time was point my finger.

28

"Right, right. On point. So my friend kept in touch with this fellow even after he was released. By coincidence, the guy settled in St. John's. He told my friend that he swore he saw you in town one day."

I sat in silence for a moment. Saw me in town? Me, in my silver wig and thick glasses and beard?

There had been a few times over the years when I'd felt as though someone had been watching. When I caught a pair of eyes that lingered a bit too long on my face. I'd always chalked it up to paranoia. Damn. As they say, just because you think people are watching you, it doesn't mean they aren't.

"And what did you do with that information?"

Brent looked a little embarrassed.

"I hired a PI in St. John's to look out for you. In your disguise, like the other fellow described. Kevin's No Frills."

"You paid a guy to sit in a grocery store all year?"

"No, no, of course not. I just hired him for the week the con said he saw you. I figured if you were staying somewhere isolated, you'd have to stock up, and you probably did it the same week every year."

He sure looked proud of himself. I was surprised by his ingenuity.

"That's actually pretty smart for a dumbass," I said.

"Well, the PI was the one who suggested—"

"And he knows you found me?"

Brent looked confused.

"He was the one who found you. He followed you up here and called me to give me directions."

"So that's who the burglar was," I mused.

"Pardon?"

"We had us a burglar a few nights ago. Or at least, we thought that's what he was. Guess he was your PI instead."

Brent nodded eagerly. "Maybe. Though I'm surprised he would come into your house."

I shrugged. "Maybe he was after my teacup too?"

"Well, *Paul*, let's face it, you *are* the most famous serial killer in Canada. Lots of places in the U.S., too. They even made a movie and some television..."

If only he hadn't pushed. He was some stunned, that kid. Didn't even notice the look on my face as he prattled on about my crimes. The ones I did, the ones they say I did but wasn't convicted for.

"There are lots and lots of people who believe you never should have been paroled. There were quite a few protests against it. Did you know that?" Brent asked.

He still thought we were having a conversation.

"I did know that. I got attacked quite often, both inside and outside."

"I read that! Can I quote you when I write the story?"

"Lad, you can quote me all you like when you write the story."

"I can't believe it! You are not what I expected at all."

"What did you expect?"

He paused, a look of embarrassment flashing through his eyes. He even blushed a little.

"A monster?" I guessed. "Not a harmless old man who serves you tea and lassy buns?"

"Well, you did slap me and you threw the cup at me, but...well, I didn't think you'd let me write the story, to be honest."

"Oh me nerves, you got me drove," I said so quietly that he kept on flapping his mouth.

"People are going to go nuts for this story. My dad will have to promote me, and I'll be a real reporter. Probably take over his job when he retires."

"Do you think people will change their minds about letting me out when they read how old and harmless I am now?" I asked.

"I do. I can write it for sympathy if you like. Explain a few things if you want me to."

"Explain that I didn't do half of what they claimed, you mean?"

"Sure, if that's your story, I will tell it."

I stared at his small, petty lips with their satisfied smirk. The mouth that formed a silent O when I broke his neck.

"Well the story would be wrong," I said to his truly dead eyes. "Once you have a monster caged, you should keep him there. Or keep him away from people. Let an outlier be."

The silence was perfect.

Miss Kitty came out of hiding and began to lap up her tuna.

The kid wasn't as much work as the burglar. That fella was a big bugger. Belatedly, I felt a grudging admiration for him, too. He'd never let on that he was a PI. Nor did he rat out the kid. Maybe he knew there'd be no tickets out of the harbor, so he kept himself to himself.

I figure I will only have to do this one more time when I pay a visit to my old pal from prison in St. John's. Good thing, too. I'm getting too old for such excitement.

And Marvin's getting too old for such rich food. I think I mentioned that pigs make great pets. They'll eat whatever's on offer.

About Catherine Astolfo

Catherine Astolfo is an award winning author, mainly mystery. In 2012, she won the Arthur Ellis for Best Crime Story. Catherine has also written five novels, two novellas and four screenplays. A Derrick Murdoch award winner, she is a Past President of Crime Writers of Canada.

To know more about Catherine, please visit her website: www.catherineastolfo.com.

THE RANCHERO'S DAUGHTER

By Sylvia Maultash Warsh

My father, the famous psychiatrist, Sebastian de Aguilar, was dying at the age of 62. I had taken over his patients in the sanitarium he founded on the *rancho* 30 years ago. Our family still kept horses, cows and hens that wandered freely among the banana plants, to the delight of the half dozen patients. They helped in the care and feeding of the animals, an integral part of the treatment at our facility. My father understood that it soothes the mind to think about someone other than oneself.

He was a pioneer in this kind of therapy, where patients and animals are brought together for the benefit of both. I myself was cheered by a tiny dog who adopted me on the street a few years ago. She was too straggly to have an owner, and though hesitant at first—she was not a man's dog—I took her home. I named her Luz, since she was a light in my life. I have a tendency toward melancholy, which she alleviated with a touch of her diminutive paw.

My father called me into his bedroom in the evenings to check on his patients' progress and give me direction. He would sit up in bed, leaning back against his pillows, while I pulled a chair to his bedside. My little Luz lay curled at my feet. I glanced at the old photo of my mother on the night table, the dark eyes moist despite the radiant smile. She had died when I was three.

My father's concern for his patients lasted several months. But as his illness progressed, he began to divert from this path and wandered into memory. He would relate milestones in his career: his studies in psychotherapy in Vienna, the autopsies of the nervous system he conducted in New York, his positions in the Ministry of Health at home.

One time he began in the same way, dredging out from dim memory the names of old physicians who had taken him under their wing in Zurich and Berlin. Then he stopped, the soft white curls on his head trembling. I had never seen him so weak. The disease was gnawing away at his identity, leaving behind a stranger.

"Mateo, you were not yet born when a *ranchero* in the neighboring valley started having trouble with his beautiful but insane daughter. He was a rich landowner from a distinguished Spanish family who had come to Honduras in the 1700s. Now, 200 years later, the family was in danger of disappearing, with the girl the last offspring. The *ranchero's* wife had died, so the girl lost her beloved mother and became even worse. The stepmother could not control her and came to hate her."

This was not my father talking! He had never demeaned himself with gossip.

"The girl was a beauty, but completely mad. One never knew what to expect from her. She whirled around when there was no music. She talked to the horses and cows, and claimed they talked back. She would scream for no reason, as if someone were killing her. They could not keep maids because the girl would curse them and prick them with a fork, threatening to eat them."

My brilliant father was disappearing. In his debilitated state, his low raspy voice arrived slowly, between halts.

"Such a beautiful girl, with long black hair and dark green eyes like a forest. The only creature she truly loved was her Chihuahua, Conchita, a demanding little dog who ate the shredded beef out of the girl's tortillas. She had the seamstress sew a special pocket in all her skirts so she could carry the dog around, its ugly little head poking out."

With effort, my father sat up and glanced at the Chihuahua lying at my feet. Luz lifted her fawn-colored head, alert. "Your dog could be her sister, they're so much alike."

I tried not to take offense at the comparison, and steered his mind back to the practice of medicine.

"Did her father take her to see a doctor?"

"In those days, they did not understand mental disease as we do now. They thought she was possessed by spirits. Because her father was rich, everyone pretended to overlook her behavior, but they murmured behind his back. He had his heart set on his daughter marrying the handsome son of a nearby *ranchero*. However, this family would not hear of it, having witnessed the girl's madness.

"While she was a child, her father went to the church in town every Sunday to pray for the spirits to leave her. When she turned 18, at his wit's end, he announced to the world that he would bequeath half of his land to the person who could cure his daughter's insanity. You can imagine that this offer brought all sorts of schemers to the *rancho* to try their luck. A woman came from far away who claimed to have psychic abilities. After a few hours, she gave up, saying the devils were too strong in the girl. A man who was famous for his powers of hypnosis arrived. When he put her under his spell, she became quiet and peaceful. Her father rejoiced. But as soon as the hypnosis wore off, she started to scream that someone was trying to kill her dog."

My father's voice had become so quiet I had to lean forward to hear.

"Men appeared from far and wide, their common attribute the conviction that their charm alone would break the spell of her madness. Two young men distinguished themselves from the others. One was a musician of medium height but well-muscled, who arrived carrying his guitar. Black hair and black eyes, he sang ballads of honor in war in a passionate voice that made even the lizards stop and listen.

"The other young man couldn't have been more different. Tall and fair, with well-formed limbs, he was a poet who recited his stanzas about the sky and the stars from memory. While the musician thrilled the girl with his ardent voice, the poet left her spellbound with his soft words that were laden with longing and regret. These two young men vied with each other to bring soundness to her mind, one with passion, the other with peace."

I had become absorbed in the story when heavy shoes sounded in the hall. Beatriz gave a knock at the open door. "*El Doctor* should have some tea."

A young boy whose parents worked on the estate carried in the tray. Beatriz could carry nothing but herself since, as a child, she had contracted polio, which destroyed the muscles in her legs. She moved awkwardly into the room on her crutches, pushing along her useless legs encased in leather braces that ended in solid shoes.

One of my father's first patients, Beatriz had arrived as a young woman soon after the sanitarium opened, her family not knowing what else to do with her. She was normal in every other way, though her upper body was muscular from the labor of pulling herself around. Not pretty so much as interesting, with wide nostrils and brown eyes that tended to protrude. But her small face was animated, softening the sum of the parts.

Though my grandmother, my *abuela*, had assumed the running of the household when my mother died, her severe nature precluded any affection. Beatriz took pity on a lonely child, and loved me. She was as close to a mother as I would ever know. I was the only one she had allowed to strap her into her braces, an intimate procedure that required access to her thighs. Once I was 12, we both shied away from the physical contact, and she had to struggle, herself, to lift the dead weight of her legs into the torturous contraptions.

Her brow creased as she gazed at my father, whom she worshipped. "He is tiring himself out."

I stood up, Luz suddenly awake on her tiny feet. "It's my fault."

Standing at the foot of the bed, Beatriz gave me her sardonic smile. "He enjoys your company."

I bent to kiss her on the cheek before I left the room, her powder scenting my lips. Now in her 50s, she was still vain enough to apply makeup.

The next evening, my father continued the story of the *ranchero*'s daughter. By this time, I knew he was failing quickly and was content just to listen to his voice.

"The girl could not make up her mind between the two young men. The musician excelled at throwing knives and twirling the lasso, while the poet milked the cows with much success, the animals entranced by his words and responding with more milk than usual.

"Both young men made a show of treating the dog with deference, knowing the girl's attachment to her. Neither of them knew the reason for the attachment—the girl had somehow come to believe the spirit of her dead mother lived in the dog. When she asked Conchita for advice, people didn't understand that she was talking to her mother. When she gave Conchita the best pieces of meat from her plate, she was feeding her mother. And the dog was a lifesaver. Once, when the girl didn't recognize her father and thought he was the devil, Conchita kept her from attacking him with a knife.

"It happened to be the season of banana fruiting. The poet had never witnessed the harvest and was loath to chop off the heart that sits beneath the banana clusters. You have seen its magenta blossom that resembles a heart, heavy with unopened flowers of baby plants inside. The new green bananas grow from it in clusters above, like a crown. But the energy required to open the unborn flowers within the heart keeps the new bananas hard and green. The old heart must be chopped off to allow the bananas to ripen. Just as I must die and you shall continue in my place."

Before I could respond to this he went on.

"The musician had no qualms about cutting off the heart of each plant with his sharp knife. The magenta blossom fell into the dry banana leaves littering the ground below, clear sap dripping from the stalk.

"The girl was greatly agitated by the keen competition between the two young men, and paced along the rows of banana plants, lamenting to Conchita. They saw the girl bent over her skirt, conferring with the dog, finally clapping her hands with pleasure at some resolution. The dog, it seemed, had an idea which the girl thought brilliant. She told the two young men to stand six feet apart in front of her amid the dry banana leaves. Then she lifted Conchita from her pocket with one hand, placing her on the ground. 'Conchita will choose between you. With her dog instinct, she can see into your hearts better than I.' The two men were shocked that their future was to be determined by a dog!

"Then the musician started addressing the Chihuahua in his sing-song voice. 'Here, Conchita, you know I'm the best one. I've seen you sway to my music.' He waved his hand at the dog to approach. She sniffed the air, then pranced toward him, her tail raised high. When he put his hand out to pick her up, she opened her little jaws and bit down hard. He held up his bloody hand, screaming, 'You bitch! You're just as crazy as she is!'

"With blood dripping down his arm, he lifted the little dog into the air by her neck and proceeded to choke her with his good hand. She yipped a few times, then her tiny eyes closed.

"The girl shrieked. She thrashed around in the huge dry leaves on the ground and found the musician's knife. With strength beyond her size, she plunged it into his heart.

"Immediately, he dropped the dog. He stared at the girl in silence before sinking to the ground.

"The poet was appalled and relieved at the same time. The girl bent beside the lifeless dog, weeping, inconsolable."

Luz gazed at me, her bulging brown eyes fraught with terror. How could she know what was being said?

"The poet lifted the tiny body of the dog, laying it in the crook of his arm. He pressed his fingers down on her chest rhythmically, once a second for a minute. Then he opened her muzzle with one hand and bending over, blew gently into her mouth.

"Time stood still. The girl held her breath. Conchita's furry little chest moved. She opened her eyes and blinked. She tried to yip but only a squeak came out. She was alive!"

Luz growled in her throat with relief.

"The poet buried the musician in an overgrown field on the estate. When the girl's father asked where the musician was, she said he had gone home because she had chosen the poet. She was not cured, but was quieter because she loved the poet and knew he loved her."

My father stopped. He leaned his head back against the pillows, his face ashen.

Beatriz pulled herself into the room on her crutches, alarmed. I had been so enrapt by the story I hadn't heard her heavy shoes in the hall.

"Sebastian," she whispered near his ear. But he could no longer hear.

I held his hand while he slipped away. I wept into my pillow all night, Luz whimpering beside me.

***

After the funeral, when the visitors had left, I found Beatriz crawling on the floor in the hall near my father's room. I placed a warning hand on Luz, whom I was carrying in one arm.

I had not seen Beatriz creeping along the floor for years. When I was young, she would sometimes get into a funk about the braces and how they chafed her skin; it was easier sometimes not to put them on. But then she was reduced to crawling on the ground like a lizard. She didn't care that a child saw her pulling her dead weight along with her arms. Now I was embarrassed for her.

She was heading back to her room. I waited until she reached it. When I heard her door close, I gave her a moment before putting down the dog and knocking.

She called for me to enter. I found her upon the settee, her face flushed from the exertion. I brought her braces toward her, but she shook her head.

"I loved him, you know."

I sat down on the edge of the bed nearby. "I know." Luz jumped onto the settee and began to lick Beatriz's face. A large tear rolled down her cheek.

"The story he was telling you—" She bit her lip. "It was not just a *ranchero*'s daughter. It was Adelita."

"Adelita! But that was my mother's name."

"Yes. Your mother."

I blinked at her, not comprehending.

40

"She was a beauty. But quite mad."

"My mother?"

She nodded.

"Then—the story was about her?"

She just looked at me and I understood. My head was spinning. I thought of the photo of the beautiful young woman on my father's night table, how little I knew about her. He had never talked about her. I racked my brain, trying to recall the details of the story.

"Then—who was the poet?"

She shook her head as if I were blind. "It isn't so difficult." When I didn't respond, she said, "Your father."

I sucked in a breath and started to cough.

"He had no more time for poetry after the *ranchero* sent him to medical school in the city. The *ranchero* knew your father had a gift for seeing into people's hearts. When Adelita danced to the music in her head, your father danced with her. I think after a while he heard it too. She seemed at peace when she was with him, and the *ranchero* thought your father could do more for her if he studied. Your father loved her more than life itself and would do anything for her. When he finished medical school, he opened the sanitarium here. He thought she was improving. You were born, and she loved you very much."

Dear little Luz could see my distress. She jumped down from the settee and stood in front of me, begging to be picked up. When I obliged, she lay down on my lap, not taking her eyes off my face.

"But she was afraid of what she might do to you. She couldn't always control herself, and she was terrified that she might… well, she had killed a man once. She was always whispering to Conchita—in her mind, her mother— for help to restrain herself.

"But when Conchita died, an old dog at 17, Adelita beat her breast as if her real mother had died again. She feared for you, that there would come a day when she would look at you and see the devil, and there would be no Conchita to keep you safe from her." Beatriz stopped.

"Please go on."

She shook her head.

"Please." I dreaded what she would say.

She took in a deep breath. "I envied her that she could walk, but she was more broken than me. One day she walked to town, climbed up to the steeple of the church...and jumped off. She did it to protect you."

A sob caught in my throat. I had lost not only my father, now I was losing a mother I had never known. I tried to compose myself. "He told me she died from heart disease."

"He could not tell you the truth."

Tears coursed down my face. Luz gazed at me with moist brown eyes. I was stunned to find they were not dog eyes, but glistened with a mother's tears, a mother's love. A shiver skipped across the back of my neck. My mother had sacrificed herself for me. Such love vanquished time, transfiguring flesh and bone, to land before me.

Little Luz finally lay her head down on her paws and let herself sleep, now that I understood. Such a tiny body, such a towering spirit.

About Sylvia Maultash Warsh

Sylvia Maultash Warsh, born in Germany to Holocaust survivors, writes the Dr. Rebecca Temple mysteries. The second in the series, *Find Me Again*, won a Mystery Writers of America Edgar Award for best Paperback Original and was nominated for two Anthony Awards at the Bouchercon World Mystery Convention in 2004. Her fourth novel, *The Queen of Unforgetting*, was chosen by Project Bookmark Canada for a plaque installation in Midland, Ont., in 2011. She also published *Best Girl*, a Rapid Reads novella in 2012. Her short story, "The Emerald Skull," from the anthology *Thirteen*, was nominated for a Crime Writers of Canada Arthur Ellis Award in 2014.

Sylvia has recently completed *The Book of Samuel*, a historical novel set in 1840s' Washington, D.C., and Virginia. She also teaches writing to seniors.

www.sylviawarsh.com

www.sylviawarsh.blogspot.ca

Facebook

Mesdames of Mayhem

To Bart
Friend of my youth
love from
Lynne

THE LION KING

By Lynne Murphy

Lynne Murphy

The Woman should not have called me Mopsy.

My first human, Daniel, called me Simba, a lion's name, a proper title for a member of the Royal House of Abyssinia. Mopsy is a name for a tabby, something meek and helpless. I have never been helpless.

Daniel understood that I was his equal. I came to live with him as a kitten. His female offspring thought he was lonely after his mate died and brought me to him.

Daniel looked at me and said, "An Abyssinian cat. I hear they are as intelligent as Siamese and not nearly as noisy. Thank you, Sarah."

Daniel and I were very comfortable together for five years. We would go for walks most evenings and he would tell me about Abyssinia, now called Ethiopia, and about the importance of lions there. Their emperor was called The Lion of Judah. Then one day Daniel collapsed on the floor, and I couldn't wake him up, no matter how hard I licked his closed eyes. At last I remembered the collar he wore around his neck. Sarah and he had talked about it. I pressed the button with my paw. Then people phoned and banged on the door, but it was too late.

Sarah took me to the shelter with tears in her eyes. "I would love to keep him but my kids are allergic," she told the woman at the door. "I understand you don't…get rid of them, even if they're not adopted." The woman patted Sarah's paw. "Don't worry—he's a beauty. And he's still young. We'll find a good home for him. It'll probably take just a few days."

In fact, the Woman and her friend came the next day. I took against the Woman right away. She looked soft, but not pillowy soft—more like the softness of unbaked dough. And she had a smell of illness about her. She wore a collar around her neck like Daniel's. I liked her friend Rose better. Her name reminded me of our garden, Daniel's and mine. But I understood from their talk that she already had a companion cat from the shelter. The Woman was there because her own cat had died not long before, of old age. So that at least was a point in her favor.

On the way home in Rose's car, the Woman said, "I'm going to call him Mopsy the Fourth."

"Oh, Betty," Rose said, "Mopsy's a name for a female. They said his name is Simba. Why not call him that?"

"No. I want to honor my other Mopsies. I've had cats called Mopsy for nearly 60 years and I couldn't adjust to a cat with another name."

And what about me? Why was I expected to be the one to adjust? I resolved to show my distaste for the name by not coming when I was called.

The Woman (I was still calling her that in my head, even when I learned that her name was Betty) had a very nice house, with lots of corners to hide in. It was warm, and there were windowsills where I could sit and look out or sleep when the sun came in. Another good place was the top of the refrigerator, which was also warm. I could keep an eye on the Woman from there. My litter box was very convenient, in the toilet room off the kitchen.

Rose lived next door and sometimes her cat, Bobby, and I looked at each other through the windows. I had no longing to go outdoors while the snow was on the ground.

The Woman found out quickly that I liked dry food and not the nasty canned stuff. She left me a big bowl every morning so I could snack during the day as I preferred. I trained her to play the fetch game with a catnip mouse. She learned to throw it for me, and I would pounce on it while it was still in the air and pretend to kill it. Then I would bring it back to her so that she could throw it again. She got quite fond of the game, and sometimes I had to hide the mouse to stop her from playing.

She tried to get me to sit on her lap, but there was always the smell of illness about her. Sometimes I wanted to bite her, it was so strong. Shut in the house as we were, with the windows closed, it could be overwhelming.

Then spring came. I sniffed it in the air and asked to go outside. When the Woman understood what I wanted, she shook her head. "I don't let my cats go outside, Mopsy. The cars are such a danger, and there may be dogs running loose. Come, let's play with Mousie."

I stalked away with my tail in the air. Daniel had let me go out in the garden. He knew I was too intelligent to run in front of a car and as for dogs—stupid noisy things, always peeing and leaving their scat in the streets for their owners to pick up—who was afraid of them when there were trees to climb everywhere?

One day I saw One Eye, a cat I knew from my days with Daniel. He had come into our garden uninvited, but after I showed him who was boss, we became friends. He lived in a colony of cats in the ravine and asked me to join them, but I couldn't leave my friend. One Eye called to me now through the window, saying, "Come outside and chase birds," but the Woman wouldn't open the door.

I watched closely, hoping to slip out. She seemed to dislike the outdoors. She didn't even go out to work in the garden. The weather grew warmer; there were birds and small animals outside. It was torture watching them through the window, not being able to get at them.

"I have to keep my eye on Mopsy and not let him get out," I heard the Woman telling Rose. "I've never had a pet that was so wild to be outside." A pet! We shared the same house, and I played Fetch with her and Mousie. That didn't make me a pet. I was so angry that I scratched her favorite chair. That was a mistake.

"I'm going to have to have him declawed," the Woman said to Rose. "That was my mother's chair."

"Can't you get him a scratching post?" Rose asked. "Bobby has one, and he uses it."

"No, he has to learn to behave if he's going to live with me."

I wasn't going to live with her if I could get outside. But without my claws, how would I survive?

The weather got even warmer, and Rose told us she was taking a trip to visit her offspring. The Woman was to go in every day to feed Bobby. I thought that might give me more chances at the door, and I made up my mind to be prepared. Once I got outside, I would run and run. I wouldn't let them catch me. But the first day, she shut the kitchen door while I was in there eating and then went next door. I had no chance to escape.

That night, the Woman went upstairs to take her bath. I had heard Rose talking to her about this habit of cleaning herself in the tub. "You'd be better to take showers. You'll get stuck someday and have to call for help."

"I don't like showers. Never feel clean with them. And I always have my alarm necklace close by. I leave it on the toilet where I can reach it from the tub."

"Well, if you want a lot of big, handsome hunks of firemen looking at you naked in the tub…"

What did tubs do that made you need help? Daniel had always taken showers so he must have known the danger. I decided to find out and followed the Woman upstairs that night. There she was, sitting in the tub. It was not a pretty sight. All that soft white, doughy flesh. Rolls and rolls of it. "Hello, Mopsy," she said. "Come to see me take my bath? That's something new." I jumped up on the toilet seat, where, sure enough, the alarm collar was sitting. The smell of illness was very strong. After washing herself all over with a piece of cloth, the Woman put both her hands on a bar at the side of the tub and tried to push herself up. Nothing happened. She tried again.

"Damn," she said, after several tries. "I'm in trouble. Move over, Mopsy. I need to get at that alarm."

Something went *ping* in my head. I gave the collar the teeniest push with my paw, and it fell off the toilet seat on the side away from the tub. Then I looked at her and meowed triumphantly.

"Now look what you've done," she said. "You'll have to fetch it for me, Mopsy. Fetch. Like with Mousie."

I jumped down from the toilet seat, and her face brightened. "Good little Mopsy," she said. I turned my back and stalked out of the room. It took her some time to realize that I wasn't coming back. That was when she started to cry for help. But the bathroom was on the second floor and its window was closed.

I knew how to open the cupboard where we kept my food. And there was drinking water in the downstairs toilet. Bobby next door didn't seem to be so lucky. He sat in the window mewing at me, but I all I could do was shrug my shoulders. I did not go back upstairs.

On the fourth day, the phone began to ring, every half hour or so. I could hear the messages Rose was leaving. "Betty, is something wrong?" "Betty, please pick up the phone," and finally, "Betty, I'm calling 911."

The firemen and police came knocking at the door just like with Daniel. I heard them talking to each other. "The dispatcher was told she's a diabetic. Maybe in a coma." And then, "Guess we're going to have to break it down."

They came charging in and stopped, wrinkling their noses at the smell, which had gotten rather strong in the house over the past few days. One of them said, "Look out, there's a cat." But I was out the door in a flash.

I called to Bobby as I went past. He was sitting in his window looking terrified. Rose would have told the police about him, I thought. They'd rescue him after they dealt with the Woman.

I didn't stop running until I was blocks away. Then I hid under a hedge in the warm dirt. It was a little lonely, and I wished I had brought Mousie for company.

But I remembered the cat colony One Eye had told me about. I would follow my nose and find it. I would walk in among them with my head high and announce, "The Lion of Judah is here. I am Simba of the Royal House of Abyssinia, destroyer of tyrants. Do not arouse my wrath."

I began to purr, thinking about it. I just had to wait till it got dark. Lions are in their element in the dark.

About Lynne Murphy

Lynne Murphy is a retired journalist whose short stories have appeared in the Mesdames of Mayhem anthologies, *Thirteen* and *13 O'Clock* as well as *The Whole She-Bang* anthologies by Sisters in Crime. Many of her stories feature the comic adventures of a group of elderly ladies who reside in the same condo building.

She is a founding member of the Toronto chapter of Sisters in Crime and the blogmistress for the Mesdames of Mayhem.

MAD DOG AND THE SEA DRAGON

By Lisa de Nikolits

We met at an art gallery one lazy afternoon.

"You and me, we could be listening to Frankie singing at The Desert Inn," he said with a sideways grin. "I always dress like this, what's your excuse?"

We were standing shoulder to shoulder and I turned to face him. I let it show that I liked what I saw. He was a straight split between Chazz Palminteri and Anthony "Mad Dog" Esposito, whose stark black-and-white photograph I had been admiring on the wall.

"This man never really left the jungle," the caption under the photograph read. "*New York Daily News*, 1941. Picture credit: Weegee."

"He was nuts," I said, gesturing to Mad Dog.

"Not as much as he would have liked to be. Him and his brother pleaded insanity to try to get off a murder charge. They barked and hit their heads on the table at the trial, they howled and cried and behaved like animals for the whole thing."

"So that's why they called him Mad Dog?"

"Nah. The New York police commissioner called him and his brother 'mad dog killers' for what they did. They killed a man in an elevator for a few hundred bucks, and then they ran out into the street and started shooting everybody. That's the part that was nuts. William, the younger brother, shot a cop, and then a taxi driver tried to save the cop. Then he—the taxi driver—got shot in the throat, but he lived, and the cab company got him a new car for his troubles."

He paused to take a breath. "The whole Esposito family was hoods. The father had done time, the third brother was in prison, the two sisters were thieves. But the mother was behind the whole thing. Mothers. The root of all evil, if you ask me."

He fell silent and turned to look at Mad Dog Esposito again. I thought I had lost him, and I struggled to think of something to say. I panicked. Things had seemed to be going really well, but now they had come to a grinding halt. My sister had given me a bunch of lines to use but I couldn't remember any of them. My mind was a complete blank, and I felt close to tears. I was going to ruin this before it even started. To my relief, he picked up the thread of our conversation.

"Look at Ma Barker," he said, turning back to me. "I don't care what they said, she made her boys and her husband do what they did. She led that gang, I don't care what anybody said about her being innocent. And Violet Kray, Ronnie and Reggie's mother. It was all her fault, too. She used to dress Reggie and Ronnie up like little girls after her baby girl died. No wonder they were both bisexual paranoid schizophrenics. Violet killed Reggie's wife, Frances, and made it look like a suicide. Mothers are behind most gang wars and crime. Women. You can't live with them, you can't live without them."

He shot a glance at me and gave a shrug as if he were about to turn and leave. I fired a question to stop him.

"What happened to the Mad Dog brothers?"

"Their pathetic attempts to look crazy didn't work. He and his brother were electrocuted in 1942."

He looked angry about something, and once again I felt like I had ruined the great start to our conversation and I frantically fished around for a way to get us back on track.

"I love these photographs," I said in my most practiced sultry voice, and I could see his mood lift again. His shoulders relaxed, and he smiled. It was a halfway twisted smile; I wondered if he practiced it in front of a mirror.

"Yeah," he said. "Weegee. Great photographer. His real name was Arthur Fellig. He got his nickname after the Ouija board for his weird way of knowing where to be when a story broke. He said it was just in his blood."

"You're a wealth of fascinating information," I purred. Why couldn't I remember what my sister had told me? We had practiced often enough. But all I could think of was cigar smoke and Paco Rabanne cologne. Could you even get Paco Rabanne anymore? Obviously, yes.

"Paco Rabanne," I said, and he smiled and straightened his tie. His suit was charcoal pinstripe and he had a blue tie and matching folded handkerchief sticking out of his pocket. His shirt was crisp white, and he shot his cuffs, giving me a glimpse of gold cuff links.

"Yeah. So what's a dame like you doing in a joint like this?"

I smoothed my form-fitting red dress over my hips and made sure my chiffon scarf was draped just so. I was wearing six-inch heels, and I was still only eye level with his chest; this man was a linebacker.

"I could ask the same of you," I said, looking up at him, trying for coy. "You look more like a businessman than an art aficionado." I figured he'd like feisty and he did.

"Well, you gotta love Weegee," he said. "He used to say the easiest kind of a job to cover was a murder because the stiff would be lying on the ground. He couldn't get up and walk away or get temperamental. He would be good for at least two hours." He laughed like this was the funniest thing. "He also said, 'Murder is my business.' I can relate."

His last sentence sent chills up my spine, but I forced myself to smile, full wattage, trying for Jessica Chastain if she'd been a star in the late '50s.

He grinned and moved closer to me, and I figured I was in. But I didn't have big boobs. A guy like this, he'd want big boobs. I'm tall, with a good round ass, a tiny waist and long legs with slender calves and finely turned ankles, if I say so myself. But there's no getting away from the fact that my boobs are like teacups. I sighed.

"Bored of me already?" he asked, one eyebrow raised.

I shook my head. "My boobs are too small for a guy like you," I said, and he gave a sharp bark of laughter.

"See, I knew I liked you already," he said. "You tell it like it is, no beating around the bush. Hey, I wouldn't worry about it. My wife's stacked, double D, and I don't much care for her."

His wife. I shut the whole thing down with a look and turned away, but he grabbed my elbow.

"Don't be like that," he said and he held my hand between both of his. His hands were enormous and slightly damp.

"This is nuts," I said, my voice breathy like Marilyn's. "I met you like three seconds ago. What's with the electricity between us?"

He grinned and pulled me closer.

"Maybe it's Mad Dog Esposito getting me so excited," I whispered in his ear. "I'll be honest. I have a crush on crazy criminals. This is the third time I've come to see this exhibit, and now you're here."

He caressed my palm and I leaned into him, my eyes shut, my breath coming fast.

"Crazy criminals aren't all they're made out to be," he said, but I only half heard him. The Paco Rabanne, his touch—the whole situation was making me feel dizzy. For a moment, I was worried that I was going to faint.

"Oh, we'll have ourselves some fun, you and me," he said, and all I could do was nod.

"You want to go someplace?" he asked.

I nodded, and that's how it all started. Me, letting him know that I wanted him, with Mad Dog leaning over my shoulder, and this man, all big and handsome, and the gallery lighting throwing shadows like cloaks and daggers.

But he was a gentleman. He took me for coffee. The place was deserted except for us.

"Tell me about you," he said while I dipped my finger into cappuccino foam and licked it clean.

"I was born into the wrong era," I said. "In my real life, I'm a late night janitor in a high-rise office. Believe me, you'd have a healthy fantasy world if that was your life too. I spend my spare time and money, not that there's much of either, sifting through thrift stores looking for garments from a better time. I've got quite the wardrobe by now."

"Girl like you should have new clothes," he said. "Shiny. Stylish, yes. But new."

I shrugged. "It is what it is," I said. "No use in complaining. And you? Tell me about you."

He was silent. "I've gotta be careful," he said. "My life's complicated. My work, my family, it's all complicated. I've got a wife, like I said, but let's not talk about her. She's a piece of work, but let's not go there. I've got a daughter. The apple of my eye."

He dug out his wallet and showed me a picture of Anne of Green Gables—red hair, braids, freckles and all.

"Isn't she a beauty?" he said. "God help the boy who lays a hand on her. She's only 10 years old, so I'm okay for a while. I wish I could lock her up in a tower forever, keep her safe from the world."

"She's pretty," I said. Kid looked like she thought her dad was Santa and the Easter Bunny all in one.

"Enough about me," he said, "I want to know more about you."

I felt like I had run out of things to say, and I hesitated. But luckily for me, he looked at his watch. "Oh darn. Listen, babe, I gotta run. Can I give you a ride somewhere?"

"I'm good," I said. "I'll catch the streetcar."

"Nah, let me give you a ride. But listen, come here, you're driving me nuts. I'm giving you some warning here. I'm going to kiss you, babe. I can't help myself. It's kismet that we met like we did."

"So stop talking already and kiss me," I said, and he did. We were locked into each other when a loud nasal voice broke the moment.

"Get a room, people," the voice said. We broke apart and looked up to see the skinny teenage barista standing there, hands on his hips. "Don't you think you guys are too old to be deep-throating it in a public place?" He grinned at us, a stupid goofy smile, not a care in the world.

My guy stood up and adjusted his suit. Next thing, the kid was crumpled on the floor, trying to breathe.

"What's wrong, kid?" my guy growled. "You can't handle a punch from a geriatric like me, huh? Come on, babe, let's get out of here."

We left the guy on the floor and I tottered after my new boyfriend, wondering if I really could handle what I had gotten into.

He gave me a ride home and when I updated my sister, she seemed satisfied.

"I told you," she said. "We're gonna land the big fish this time."

***

The next time we met, it was at the bar at the Four Seasons hotel. He had booked a room on the 14th floor, with a view of the city that stretched for miles.

"I hope you don't think I'm presumptuous," he said as we rode up on the elevator. "I have to watch who I'm seen in public with, I'm sure you understand."

"Of course," I said but my heart was hammering in my chest like a nail gun.

When we got to the room, he ordered champagne and an array of desserts.

"My mother watches what I eat like a hawk," he said, biting down on a cream-filled éclair and washing it down with champagne. "Now my wife, she wouldn't dare say a word to me but mothers can say whatever they like. You never get out from under the thumb of your mother."

"Never, ever talk about his mother," my sister had told me. "Italian matriarch, she's like the Virgin Mary and the Queen of England all rolled into one. The woman is a saint to him. I met her once. She was like Hannibal Lecter in drag. She's more dangerous than I can tell you. When he talks about her, just nod."

I nodded.

"You're not eating, babe?" My guy drew my attention back to the spread in front of us. He was chewing on a custard Danish, crumbs flying everywhere.

"Don't want to ruin my figure," I said, running my hands over my waist suggestively. Actually, I could eat like a horse and never put on an ounce, as my sister constantly reminded me, as if that were my fault. If she even walked past a muffin, she gained a pound. But I was sick with nerves now and couldn't eat a thing. I couldn't even take more than a sip of champagne. What if I didn't get the sex right? What if he didn't like me?

"I'm nervous," I blurted out. "I'm worried you won't like me or find me attractive. I just want you to like me."

"Oh, honey." He came over to me and pulled me up out of the chair I had been sitting in. "You have no idea how much I like you already. I haven't been able to think about anything except you. I can't concentrate. I can't think straight. Come here. Let me show you just how much I want you."

And he did. And it turned out the size of my boobs was perfectly fine, thank you very much, and when he cupped my ass in his big hands, it seemed like it was all working out just like we had planned.

I lay on my side as he slept next to me, his arm draped over my waist and I looked at the stretched-out city below and thought that maybe for once, I really did have the world at my feet.

***

"I just don't want to screw it up," I said to my sister when I was getting ready for a date. "What if he gets bored of me? What if I say something stupid?"

"You can handle it," my sister said when I told her my concerns. "You just don't think you can. Why someone with your looks has such low self-esteem is beyond me. Let me tell you, if I had your looks, I'd own the world. Frickin' own it." I had lost count of how many times she had told me that in my life. "The mistake you made in the past," she continued, "was dating good-looking losers who folded like cheap tents when it counted. This time, just listen to me, do what I tell you and you'll come out the winner."

I nodded. I didn't agree with her that I had low self-esteem. And I was no floozy. I had only fallen in love with one guy and he had let me down badly, that much was true.

But you couldn't help who you fell in love with; it just happened.

My sister had always been more like a mother to me than a sister.

When I was five, my father came home and found my mother passed out on the sofa, drunk. He sat down next to her and he looked at me. I was sitting on the floor, waiting for my sister who was making me chocolate milk and toast for supper.

"I can't take it anymore," my father said to me, and I remember exactly how he said it. He was very matter-of-fact, very calm.

Then he turned back to my mother and pressed a cushion to her face, pushing down on her while her legs thrashed and flailed and drummed against the arm of the sofa.

I wet my pants and sat there in a puddle while my father killed my mother and my sister made my supper in the kitchen. She didn't hear a thing.

"I'm sorry you had to see that," my father said. Then he got up and left me alone with my mother, who was staring straight at me with bloodshot eyes. Not that bloodshot was anything new.

I don't know how long it was before my sister came in with my supper and when she saw my mother lying there, she dropped the toast and the chocolate milk and the brown puddle spread into my pee. I just looked at my sister and stuck my thumb in my mouth.

"Where's Dad?" she asked urgently, and I shook my head.

She ran to the bedroom and was gone a long time. When she came out, she said she had found him and needed to phone the cops. He had hanged himself in the bedroom. I remember wondering why she had been in there so long with his dead body, but I couldn't ask her because I had forgotten how to speak.

It took me a long time to talk again after the murder-suicide, and that's when my sister became my mother, my best friend and my guardian angel. We went to live in a bunch of foster homes, and I escaped into books, reading anything I could get my hands on. I loved *Wuthering Heights* best of all. When I met Joey at one of the homes, I thought he was my Heathcliff forever. He was the love of my life. I was 16, and my life finally seemed good; I was even happy for a while. But a couple of years later, Joey got arrested for armed robbery and that was the end of that. I never stopped loving him, not for a moment, but my sister never let me see him again. I would have visited him in prison, but she wouldn't let me.

So I made up this fantasy world where I was a big movie star with elegance, grace and style. I spent hours in thrift stores, finding the right garments that a real star would wear. I practiced talking in a slow and famous way, keeping my voice lazy and even. I pictured myself on a big screen wherever I went, like the world was watching me with all my grace and loveliness, and I never let myself slip. My name is Vickie, but I changed it to Jessica, after Jessica Lange. I thought I looked a lot like her. And no one was allowed to call me Jess or Jessie. I was Jessica.

My sister's name is Glennis. And she told me all the time that I had ruined her life. But it wasn't me who ruined her life. What ruined my sister's life is that she's not like me. She's not a looker. It's like she got the opposite of everything I had. I'm tall, she's short; I'm willowy, she's a dumpling; I've got tiny tits, she's loaded. When looks were being handed out, she came out on the short end. There isn't one thing about her that is pretty. If you ask me, that's why she was so mean to me all the time. I felt bad for her.

How would I feel if I looked like she did? I'd be angry with life, too. My heart broke when I saw how people looked at her.

"Life's not fair and that's just the way it goes," she often said. But she would look at me accusingly, as if it were my fault that she wasn't pretty and had never had a man love her.

Apart from Joey—and he didn't count anymore—my sister was the only person in my life.

"Why do you need friends when you've got me?" she asked me when I made plans with schoolmates. After a few tries, I just gave up. It was easier that way.

"Do what I tell you," she said again when I told her I was worried I was going to screw things up with my guy. "I'll make sure you land this man, get him in the bag, hook, line and sinker."

***

I paid attention to what she said and worked hard. Not even a month later, my guy made me give up my job and moved me into a brand-new condo with a view of the lake. He'd never been to my place. I'd told him I shared a basement apartment with another janitor, but he hadn't cared about those kinds of details about my life.

"You don't need to be handling anybody's garbage," he said. "You're my girl now and I'll take care of you. Thing is, I got some rules. First off, you don't get to talk about my wife. Ever. Next, you do not step out on me. Thirdly, you tell me where you are, 24/7. Fourth. Do not steal from me. If you need money for something, you just got to ask me. You wear my gifts, you do not sell them. Number five. You always gotta look like a million bucks and smell like a peach. I don't want to turn up and find you in your pj's with your hair from yesterday. One more thing. You're only out if I say you're out. Out of this—you and me. Never think you can skip town on me, you got that? Wait. Don't ever ask me what I do for a living. Any questions?"

"I got it," I said. "But I will ask one thing of you and if you agree, then you've got yourself a deal."

He raised an eyebrow. "Yeah?"

"I want a leafy sea dragon," I said. "It won't be cheap. It won't be easy to get. And it will cost you about 10 grand."

"A leafy sea dragon," he repeated, and smiled.

"There's one at the aquarium," I said, "I can show you."

"I know what a leafy sea dragon is," he said. "Looks like a fancy long seahorse in a wedding dress. They're special, just like you, babe, beautiful and delicate. Sure, I'll get you one."

"How do you know what it is?" I asked.

"I take my kid to the aquarium a lot," he said. "She loves them, too. You've got good taste."

I wasn't sure why I asked for a leafy sea dragon. Maybe I thought there was no way he could get me one, and that my asking would shut down this crazy thing once and for all.

I was glad I never told my sister about asking for the leafy sea dragon because she would have killed me. She would have said I was self-sabotaging and ruining everything.

Now, here's the thing. My sister has worked for my guy for 10 years and he still can't remember her name. She works in the accounts department, faithfully handling all kinds of stuff and no matter how many hours she logs, or how much money she saves him or how many secrets she keeps, he can never remember her name. He calls her *doll* or *cookie* but in 10 years, he has never once said her name and finally, one day, she had enough and that's when she got the idea for us to work him over.

She had realized that the girlfriend on the side was no longer in the picture and that it was time for him to get himself a newbie. It was all her idea. She knew all about previous girlfriends, all Jessica Rabbit look-alikes that he'd kept in gilded cages. Clothes, cash, jewelry—my sister said we could collect a real good stash and head to Florida. Hundreds of thousands of dollars, she said. And I didn't have to do anything except look pretty.

"Nice work if you can get it," she said, sounding bitter like always. I wondered if she had a crush on my guy, if that was really why she wanted to get me in to score the big bucks. Maybe it was her way of getting revenge. But wasn't she putting me in danger? Would she do that?

"If they all had it so good, why did they leave?" I asked.

My sister gave me an even look. "Who says they left? You'll have to be careful. But don't worry. I know how his timing works. I'll get you out when the time comes. And who knew all your bargain basement '50s clothes will actually be good for something. All this time, I thought your obsession with dressing like a vintage calendar girl was a waste of time and money. But it's going to turn out to be perfect for what we need."

Her admission didn't make up for her nasty comments every time I had brought home a new five-dollar gem of a dress or a pair of shoes that fit me just so, but I held my tongue. If we scored big-time, it wasn't worth arguing about.

As luck would have it, she heard him talking about the Weegee exhibit and knew exactly when he was going to the gallery. So we came up with the plan. I got all dolled up, and next thing, Bob's your uncle, I was sitting in my gilded cage and Daisy, the leafy sea dragon, was happily waving her lacy little fins at me and floating around her 500-gallon tank.

***

My guy had no idea that I had only seen a leafy sea dragon because of him. He'd had to cancel a trip to the aquarium with his daughter and had given the tickets to my sister because he had chewed her head off about something. Even though he couldn't remember my sister's name, he'd given her the tickets.

The aquarium bored me, but when we found the sea dragon, I fell in love. There was this perfectly beautiful little creature, with her lacy fins spinning and waving, and that perfect tiny horse face was looking at me, only at me.

And there was me looking at her. I could see my reflection in the glass. I was lovely, too, exotic even, with my careful coiffure and my perfect red lipstick. And what did I have to show for it? Nothing. The sea dragon was stuck in her cage, and I was stuck in mine. My life was a cage. So what if I was beautiful? It's not like it ever got me anything except my sister's quiet rage and my heart broken.

Which is why, when my sister told me about her cockamamie plan, I agreed to it. I wanted to try to be something more than a late-night janitor with thrift store dress-up dreams. Maybe I wanted to prove to my sister that I was worth something. Or maybe I was tired of being poor. It sounded nice to have a guy look after me and not have to worry about money all the time. And it would be nice to not have to live with my sister.

To be honest, the whole thing made me feel like I was the star of a show, like I was playing a role in a Dashiell Hammett book, with shady gangsters with names like Whistler, and beautiful women who wore dresses made of crêpe de chine.

And then, when my guy popped the big question about setting me up for real, the leafy sea dragon popped into my head. I asked for her on a whim and my guy said sure, it wouldn't be easy, but for me, anything.

***

I settled into a routine pretty quickly, and it wasn't too bad at first. I got to buy all the books I wanted, and I read all the hours of the day and night. And I can't say I minded the fancy jewelry boxes that came filled with glittering gems, or the envelopes of cash that elevated my wardrobe to that of a real star.

But I wasn't in love with him, and I couldn't even find a way to like him. Sometimes when we were having sex, I felt like I was a custard Danish he was chewing on.

And it was horrible, never knowing when he was going to show up. I had to be ready, on call all the time. When I heard the sound of the key turning in the lock, my stomach clenched. He liked to surprise me by coming at all hours, like he was testing me. After a while, I couldn't even concentrate on my books. I was listening for that sound, that grinding sound that told me it was time to sit up and look happy like a good puppy.

And now, it's six months later. I am sitting here in my prison, dressed to the nines, waiting for my guy. Daisy is looking at me inquisitively, like she wants to know what's going to happen next. "I don't know," I whisper to her. "I don't know."

I try to stop myself from picking at my cuticles because my guy hates it. He says only poor drug addicts pick at themselves until they bleed. But I get a release from the pain; it helps me focus my worry and fear.

"When will it be time to get out?" I asked my sister the last time I saw her. We meet once a week in the hats-and-gloves section of the department store and talk like spies do, side by side, facing forward, pretending to be strangers who just happen to be muttering at each other, like that's not obviously weird or anything.

"Not yet," she said, trying on a pair of lamb's wool gloves.

"When is yet?" I asked. "My life is killing me."

"Poor baby," my sister said. "Living in the penthouse, being treated like a queen. Suitcases of cash to spend on whatever you want. Sex with a gorgeous man. Yeah, you've really got it tough."

Sex with a gorgeous man? I swung around to face her, not caring who might see us arguing.

"You're in love with him, aren't you?" I asked. "You've always been in love with him." I saw the hatred flare in her eyes as she looked at me.

"But why set me up with him?" I asked when I saw she wasn't going to answer me. "What good would that do you? Is it the money? You know I am saving as much as I can, for you and me, just like we planned."

She was struggling for words. I could see she was thinking half a dozen things, that she wanted to say something but couldn't find the right words.

"You and him. You deserve each other," she finally said.

"What do you mean?" I asked. "Talk to me. I don't get it."

"He thinks you love him." She laughed. "So stupid. I like to look at him and think to myself, 'Buddy, you've got no idea how you are being played, played by me! Nameless, faceless me!' What would he think he if knew?"

I felt dizzy. The department store lights seemed to swell like crazy faces, and I nearly stopped breathing.

"Do you plan to tell him somehow?" I asked, hardly able to talk. "He'll kill me. And he'll kill you."

"Like I've got so much to live for," she said. "I'm nothing but a blob. No one sees me. I don't matter to no one. I'll never be happy. I've never been happy, not once in my whole life."

"You've got me," I said. "We've got each other. We've always had each other. Through everything. You're just upset now. Think about our lives in Florida, how we'll live in the sunshine and never have to worry again. We'll be happy then, we will be."

But would we be happy? Who was I kidding? My sister was right. She would never be happy. And me? I didn't think I could find a way to be happy, either, not even with all the money in the world.

I was silent and we turned away from each other and starting touching the gloves again, picking up random pairs.

"Maybe," she finally said, "his mother will find out. If you ask me, you should be worried about her, not him. I get the feeling she doesn't approve of him having fancy girls on the side. But you know what? I like her. She stopped by the office, and we got chatting. What do they call people like her? Salt of the earth, that's it. Salt of the earth."

"Tell me," I said, struggling to get the words out, the words that had been stuck in my throat for more than 20 years, "what were you doing in the bedroom all that time with Dad's dead body?"

She stared at me. "You're asking me that now? Why now?"

"I always wondered," I said.

She shrugged. "I was letting him finish the job. He could never get anything right, our father. So I stood there and I made sure he did it right, for once."

Then she left me. She didn't say another word, just turned and left. I didn't know what to do. Would she tell my guy? Could I even go back to my apartment? But where else could I go? What else could I do? So I went home and watched Daisy float this way and that, and I tried to figure out what to do.

I can't tell Daisy what I am really thinking because I'd bet dollars to doughnuts that my guy has the place bugged. So I press my face to the glass of her tank, and I know that Daisy knows. She knows that I have no choice. I'll have to kill my guy. And I'll need to be packed and ready. I'll take all my fancy clothes, all my jewels, my stash of money. I'll leave, and I won't go to Florida. I'll go somewhere glamorous, like Los Angeles, and maybe try my hand at acting. I'll become a star, and then it will serve them right, both of them. I try to think but my head hurts, and the glass of Daisy's tank is cool and soothing against my forehead.

I'll make sure you're looked after, I tell her silently. *Don't worry. I'll never let you down.*

I don't have a phone. I'm not allowed one. I am too afraid to buy one.

I think about trying to call my sister from a pay phone. My sister hasn't met me for our drive-by hello after that terrible conversation. I walked around the hats-and-gloves section for hours on our appointed meet-up day, picking things up and putting them down, but she never showed.

I was sure she would come back and say she was sorry, that she had never meant to say the things she had said, that she loved me and our plan was a good one, and that she had just been tired that day. Maybe my guy had been rude to her and she had taken it out on me. I was so sure she would show up and tell me everything was going to be okay. But she didn't, and that's when the real terror began.

It's time to face the facts. Life's not fair, and that's just the way it goes. My sister watched my father die. I watched my mother being murdered. And now I have to rely on myself to get out of this.

I don't want to die. So I sit and watch Daisy. I know that one day I'll come up with a plan. I will kill my guy and make my great escape. I just don't have that part figured out yet.

I'm not sure how much time has passed. I have the terrible urge to suck my thumb, but I sit on my poor picked-at hands instead. All I know is that I can't remember the last time I ate, and I need to take a bath. Nerves have left me as fragrant as a marathon runner's old shoes, and my hair has passed yesterday's sell-by-date by a long shot.

Why hasn't my guy come? He was supposed to bring the fellow who cleans Daisy's tank, which is looking worryingly cloudy. The apartment is filled with dead air, and I can't explain the silence.

There's a knock at the door, and I jump up in fright. Why is my guy knocking when he's got the key? But then my heart fills with joy—it's my sister coming to say she's sorry, coming to rescue me. We'll make our big getaway together and go live our lives in the sun.

I rush to the door and pull it open. The big wide smile on my face is killed by what I see.

I've never met the woman before in my life, but I know who she is. I am looking up at my guy's mother. She's tall like him and just about as wide, and the expression on her face doesn't reassure me.

"I thought it was time we had a little visit," she said, pulling on a pair of gloves, which alarmed me even more. "Step aside, dearie, and let me in."

About Lisa de Nikolits

Originally from South Africa, Lisa de Nikolits has lived in Canada since 2000. She has a Bachelor of Arts in English Literature and Philosophy and has lived in the U.S.A., Australia and Britain. *No Fury Like That*, her most recently published work, is her seventh novel and has received rave reviews.

Previous works include: *The Hungry Mirror* (2011 IPPY Awards Gold Medal for Women's Issues Fiction and long-listed for a ReLit Award); *West of Wawa* (2012 IPPY Silver Medal Winner for Popular Fiction and a *Chatelaine* Editor's Pick); *A Glittering Chaos* (tied to win the 2014 Silver IPPY for Popular Fiction); *The Witchdoctor's Bones, Between The Cracks She Fell* (won a Bronze IPPY Award 2016 for Contemporary Fiction) and *The Nearly Girl*.

Her eighth book, *Rotten Peaches*, is scheduled to be published in 2018. All titles by Inanna Publications.

Author website: lisadenikolitswriter.com
Twitter: @lisadenikolits
Author Page: facebook.com/lisadenikolitsauthor
Goodreads: Lisa de Nikolits
LinkedIn: linkedin.com/in/lisadenikolits/

NIGHT VISION

By Mary Patterson

Malachi rolled himself over into the patch of sunlight by the front window. He was feeling rather hungry; there had been no sign of the keeper of the can opener arriving home. This was a misfortune, he felt, as his tummy rumbled gently with emptiness. Then he heard the familiar slam of the door of the old blue car, and he knew that help was on the way.

Purring, he made the usual feline obeisance by rubbing himself against the man's trouser cuffs, receiving an affectionate stroke down his back in return.

"Hungry, old guy?"

Of course he was hungry! Didn't this man know that cats should be served meals on a regular basis? He realized he'd have to give basic obedience lessons to this new man. It was such a shame that the old lady had disappeared so suddenly, just when he'd had her well-disciplined! That was the trouble with these tall creatures who inhabited his world. No consideration!

So here was Malachi, starting basic training once again. This one, however, might be more of a problem, as he seemed to disappear and reappear at odd times. Yesterday, for example, he'd hung around all day, then suddenly went out when it was very dark. He hadn't reappeared until nearly noon.

The whir of the can opener brought Malachi to the kitchen, and he wove his way around the man's trousers until he heard the welcome plop of food hitting his bowl. Sniffing, he hoped for the delicious scent of chicken, not

73

that smelly fish that sometimes was placed in front of him. That was another job he would have to work on: no fish, and not too much liver, it really gave him heartburn. But today was one of the good ones, and he wrapped himself around his bowl of Kitty Delight Chicken, fervently lapping it up in tiny bites until the bowl was glisteningly empty.

"You must have been hungry" came the ridiculous remark from above his head, and Malachi went into his prescribed routine of purring and rubbing once again.

No, not hungry, half-starved. He padded over to the litter box, where he turned his back pointedly, but he was delighted to see that his early lesson on how to request fresh bathroom products had finally sunk in. The soiled product in the litter box had been removed from near his fastidious nose and replaced with a clean refill.

Perhaps this new one wouldn't be too hard to train after all, Malachi thought, if only he would start keeping more regular hours.

The jangling ring of the telephone interrupted his thoughts. The tall one was speaking rapidly to someone, firing off questions and talking to himself as he wrote down what must have been instructions.

"Okay," he said. "You're leaving this evening?...Ten-thirty?...Yep. I'll be there....Let's see if we can catch the two of them together this time. Last evening was a total washout. Just your wife and a couple of girlfriends at another woman's house. A 'girls' night out,' I guess. They had pizza delivered, brought in beer and never left the house until 10 this morning. Maybe we'll have better luck tonight....How long are you gone for?...And she knows that?...Great. I'll try to get a few pictures if I can. Do you know what this guy drives?...Yeah, yeah, I got that....A red convertible? You're sure?...Yeah. That'll make the job easier....I hope to have some evidence for you when you get back....Luckily, it's supposed to be warmer tonight. Makes watching from a car much more comfortable....Okay. Wish me luck!"

As he hung up the phone, he turned to Malachi. "Got to get some sleep. I'm back on duty again tonight. Want to come with me? I could sure use some company out there."

Malachi purred his assent, though he was fairly sure his message wasn't understood. "Sure I'll come along, if you'll guarantee some refreshments," he meowed.

That evening, as the man donned his coat, Malachi planted himself firmly at the front door, ready for an evening's outing. That was one of the drawbacks of this new man. Malachi was never let outside for the night, his favorite time to be out on his own.

"Hey! That's right! You can be my partner tonight. Two sets of eyes are better than one, they say, and for a private eye, that goes double!"

Partner! That appealed to Malachi.

"I'll just bring along your harness in case you need an outing. A litter box in a car isn't my idea of fresh air." And the legs hurried back down the hall to the kitchen.

Don't forget the refreshments. Malachi was relieved to see a box of cat treats arrive along with the leash. He allowed the pink collar to be fastened around his neck. (What had the man been thinking? Pink?)

And then he strolled out to the old car and gracefully leapt in amongst the accumulated debris that seemed to fill much of the space: old cups of coffee, half drunk and then forgotten, and paper bags with the grease stains of quickly eaten hamburgers. And this guy was bothered by his litter box odors? Malachi sniffed disdainfully, then investigated one of the bags where a few forgotten French fries still lurked.

He curled up on an old car rug as the car started up, while the man's voice rumbled on, telling him—or was he talking to himself, Malachi wondered—about their duties for the evening. "She's been running around with this young guy from the local car dealership. Her husband wants a divorce real quick, before she knows that he's on to her, so she won't be prepared with some clever lawyer demanding a lot of alimony. Besides, it doesn't look good for a bank manager to be involved in a sordid divorce."

Malachi wasn't sure of the word *divorce*. The old lady, this guy's aunt, hadn't "run around" with anybody. She just went to work. Malachi thought she was teacher or something. She always smelled of chalk, carried many papers with her, and—most importantly—she never stayed out all night like this one did!

But this man had come quickly when they took her away in a noisy white truck he had heard someone call an ambulance, and she hadn't returned. He'd taken Malachi home with him, along with his belongings—a bowl, a cushion and a blanket, and a leash, but not a collar, as Malachi had hidden it out in the back garden one day. (He was sorry he'd done that when he saw the new substitute pink thing he was supposed to go out in! Talk about embarrassing!)

The evening started off quietly, as they drove for a half hour into a much busier area of town. The man parked the car away from a streetlamp, which pleased Malachi, as bright lights always spoiled his great night vision.

Are we getting out here? Malachi wondered, sitting up at attention, but was quickly disappointed. His driver had settled down, his head turned toward the window. He seemed to be watching the front driveway of a wide stone house. A large and luxurious silver car was parked in the driveway.

Malachi watched as the front door opened, and a rotund man with silvery gray hair emerged, carrying a small suitcase. He glanced around and, spotting their old blue car, waved briefly at Malachi's partner, who returned the gesture. A red-haired woman appeared, framed for a minute in the doorway, kissed the man perfunctorily, then disappeared back inside.

The gray-haired man opened the car door, swung the suitcase into the backseat, then drove off. The street returned to silence. Malachi and his partner settled themselves more comfortably, until a low red convertible, its radio blaring loud music, swung into the driveway.

A tall, dark-haired young man emerged from the convertible and glanced around furtively, before loping up to the door of the house and knocking. When the door swung open, the red-haired woman made another brief appearance before the two of them disappeared inside. After a short while, the lights downstairs were turned off, and the upstairs windows lit up, but only for a few minutes.

Malachi saw that his partner was busy adjusting a camera. He was obviously displeased, because he muttered something about poor lighting. Then he sank back down in his seat and eventually started to snore gently. Malachi settled himself more comfortably into the old blanket and also took a brief nap.

He was jolted awake some time later when the large silver car reappeared down the street and screeched to a stop in front of the stone house. The driver threw the car door open and hurried to the house's front door, where he started pounding noisily.

Thinking this might be important to their job, Malachi jumped into the front seat, on sharp claws which he used to good advantage to wake up his sleeping partner. Just in time to see the front door fly open and the young man emerge, pulling on his shirt as he sprinted to the red car and vaulted into the driver's seat. A moment later, the convertible's engine sprang back to life with a loud roar.

The older man moved quickly to block the red car's hasty departure. The driver swerved around him, then started up the street.

The older man ran after the convertible for a moment. He pulled something from his pocket and pointed it at the convertible. There was a loud bang and a flash— and again and again. The red car jumped the curb and slammed into a lamppost.

Everything fell silent. Up and down the street, lights came on in houses, and people, wearing assorted gowns and pajamas, emerged in little clusters.

Malachi's partner, now wide awake, jumped out of their car and ran to the red convertible. He looked inside at the figure slumped over the wheel, then shouted at the older man, "Put the gun down! He's dead! You've killed him!"

The older man yelled, "You saw me! He tried to run me down and kill me! You're my witness!"

"No, you deliberately got in the way. He was avoiding you!"

"No, no!" the older man cried. "He tried to kill me! It was self-defence. You saw it! You're a witness!"

"No, no, no! It was murder!" Malachi's owner insisted. "Give me the gun." He strode over and attempted to wrest it out of the man's hand.

A wailing sound reached Malachi's ears. A white police car swung into the street, stopped briefly at the crashed convertible, then drew up beside the two struggling figures. Two officers jumped from the squad car to separate the men.

The older man demanded to be let go, that he hadn't done anything. He kept shouting that the convertible's driver had tried to kill him by driving over him. Malachi's partner repeated, "No! You got in his way deliberately! He didn't try to run you down at all."

Malachi kept shouting, too. "He's right, he's right! You did it!" But nobody seemed to hear his voice at all.

"Listen to me! Listen! Why can nobody hear me? That's another thing I'll have to work on," complained the cat before jumping back into their car to find the bag of cat treats that had been spilled in all the excitement.

His partner eventually returned to their car and resumed his seat. He turned to Malachi. "Thanks, old man. If you hadn't woken me up in time, I might have believed that sleazebag's story. Imagine him trying to set me up as his alibi. I owe you one! Say, how'd you like to come on most of my jobs, like a partner, eh? With your night vision, we'd make a great team. Let's see. We could run the business as Four Eyes Investigations. How's that sound you to, buddy?"

Oh, night work! Malachi purred his acceptance.

But, he thought, I'd better work on my communication skills if I don't want to be just the silent partner in this business.

About Mary Patterson

Mary Patterson is the winner of the Mesdames' contest for unpublished crime fiction writers. She is a retired potter and garden columnist for community newspapers. Freedom from pottery work now leaves her time to write fiction and grow plants year round as well as planning and planting several community garden projects along with her husband. Despite creating loveable cat PI, Malachi, she's actually a dog fan!

Mary is currently finishing off a mystery novel featuring poisonous mushrooms, set in Toronto's High Park.

THE COFFEE TIN

By Melodie Campbell

The little dog had been following her ever since she bolted from the house on Wednesday night. Whenever Jess looked behind her, there it was, about ten steps back. She'd stop, and then it would stop. Wait. Wag its tail a few times. Poor thing looked awfully thin. Its predominantly white hair was badly matted. She couldn't help but feel sorry for the mutt, even though its presence made her feel pretty awful.

On Thursday, when Jess came out from the run-down basement apartment she shared with two other girls, there it was. Its black eyes shone with eagerness, and its little tail wagged fiercely.

Shit, thought Jess. *Just what I need. A reminder.* The dog had probably been there all night. It was late spring, so at least the little animal would be warm enough outside.

Jess took a closer look at it. *Male*, she noted. *Probably a Shih-poo, one of those cross-things.*

"Shoo," she said, waving her arms.

The little dog stopped wagging his tail. His ears drooped. Jess continued down the sidewalk. When she looked back at the corner, the dog was following her at a distance.

Jess decided to ignore him. Soon he would tire, and leave her alone.

But he didn't. When Jess came out of the pawn shop at midday, there he was, at the bottom of the steps, waiting. Her heart sank.

"You're like a ghost," she said to him. The eyes were not as shiny now. The little tongue panted heavily.

Needs water, Jess realized. She hesitated, looking around her. "Come on. I'll find you some."

Jess walked to the corner and crossed the street with the light. Her companion scurried after her. She vanished for a few minutes into a building. When she came out with a bag and a drink, the little dog was one store over, lapping up dirty water from a puddle on the broken pavement.

"Don't do that," Jess scolded. She took the plastic top off the paper cup. "Here's some fresh water." She offered it to the pooch. He didn't move away from the puddle.

Jess walked over to the dog and lowered the cup to his level. "Drink this," she said.

The little dog moved forward with caution, and began to lap frantically. Jess had to keep tipping the cup as the water level went down.

She tried to recall his name. Something cutesy, she remembered. Muffy? No, that was the Maltese in the corner house.

She thought back to the old woman. What name had she yelled from the top of the stairs? Lucky! That was it. *Well little guy, you haven't been lucky for either of us.*

At last, Lucky stopped drinking. Water dripped down his bedraggled chin fur. The look on the little dog's face made Jess feel like someone had reached in and scrunched her heart.

"Let's find a place to sit," she said. At the end of the block was a small parkette. Some rich person had left the corner lot to the city when they died. It wasn't much of a park. Just one wooden bench and a shabby swing set, the ancient kind that had leather straps for seats. Jess remembered playing on it when she was younger. Before her parents had divorced, and before her mother had shacked up with the creep.

Jess looked back to check that Lucky was still behind her. Then she continued to the bench and sat down. The little dog followed; he sat in front of her, just out of reach. Jess put down the water cup and opened the bag. Her right hand delved in to retrieve a cone of French fries. She picked out a long one and threw it to the dog.

He moved swiftly to gobble it down.

Jess stared at the animal. She knew what it was like to be hungry. She took a bunch more out of the cone, and scattered them in front of the dog. Lucky moved from one to the next, vacuuming them up with lightning speed.

When the French fries were finished, Jess continued to the cheeseburger. She unwrapped the wax paper and used both hands to rip the burger in half. One part she kept for herself. The other, the larger half, she put on the ground between them.

It vanished within seconds.

After that, Lucky settled on the warm grass for a lie-down. The eyes that looked up at her had changed. They were still black, but no longer dull. They shone with something like hope.

"Do you miss her, the old woman?" Jess said. The dog perked up and wagged his tail. He seemed to be saying, *I like you better.*

Lucky crept forward and put a hesitant paw on her leg. The contact seemed to crack open a door that had been shut inside Jess for a long time. She reached down and gathered Lucky up in her arms, then plunked him on the bench beside her.

"She didn't take very good care of you. Someone needs to work out those mats."

Lucky lay down on the bench, leaning up against her. Jess put her hand down to stroke the soft fur. What would become of him? He was homeless now, and in a weird Greek-tragedy sort of way, Jess was responsible for it.

She'd only meant to steal the money in the coffee tin. Everyone knew the nasty old lady kept her cash there. It should have been a quick in and out. The back door lock had been easy to pick. Jess had been quiet, but not silent enough. She hadn't counted on the old crow being in the bathroom upstairs taking a leak, instead of tucked up in bed.

She couldn't block it from her mind—the cry...the fall.

"I didn't mean for her to die," Jess said to the dog.

Lucky looked up at her with soulful black eyes. *I didn't mean to trip her on the stairs,* he seemed to say.

They snuggled closer together, each finding comfort in the warmth of the other. Jess came to a decision. She would keep the dog. It wouldn't be easy. But if she was careful—really careful—the money from the coffee tin would provide food for Lucky for a long time.

DANA'S CAT

By Rosalind Place

Hello….Jack!…No. My number's unlisted that's all….Did I? Well, sorry again, then….Twenty years, it must be….It sure was. The house goes up for sale and the next thing I know I'm walking right into you….What?…No, sorry, it's just that it's been years since anyone called me Evie….Are you? Sure, well since you have my number you can just call again when you have more time.

***

So, Cat, are you coming in at last? It's all right. You can. I even have food. Somewhere. Assuming you're not a ghost and do actually eat. Well, I have milk anyway. How's that?

Seeing you over there day after day, sitting there like a little black statue. I thought I was imagining things. You are the spitting image. It's been a little unnerving, to tell you the truth—seeing you sitting there, just when her house goes up for sale.

I'll never forget it. The sight of that cat crossing the road with a kitten in her mouth. Carrying it along to I don't know where, then going back for another one. That was almost 30 years ago and I've never seen another one like her until you—that white splotch on your shoulder. You must be related. Either that or you're a doppelgänger. A hungry doppelgänger, by the look of it.

***

Hello?…Oh. Hi again, Jack….Improving. I should be back at work by spring with any luck….No. It was a car accident. Guy drove right into me, then buggered off….The factory? Surely you knew. It's been gone for years. Walk down now and you'd never know it'd ever been there....No, you're right. Time waits for no one. I haven't seen anyone going through, but I probably won't. Everything round here goes to developers....Yes, condos mostly....One of those monster houses or maybe a low-rise....Okay, Jack. We can chat more later. Call back when you have more time.

***

Funny how he calls, but doesn't have time to talk. Funny that he calls at all, really. So, Cat, you're back for a visit. Well, for dinner, anyway. Dry or canned? My house is suddenly stocked with food, so you have a choice. How did that happen? What is it about that old place, eh? And what'll you do when they come to tear it down? They will, you know.

You make me think of Dana, the way you come across from there looking for company.

We were all at the factory back then, everyone round here—well, the men, anyway, and me. Two shifts, sometimes three. Jack managed to get straight days. I never knew how.

They'd just moved from out west, and he talked like he'd been handpicked.

I'd always hated shift work, but after they came I was glad of it. If I was on nights, I'd be getting home just as Jack was heading out, and it wouldn't be long before I'd see Dana crossing the road. She was always holding a plate of something—she was a good baker. I told her more than once she could've had her own business.

I can see her now. Tall, like Jack. But where he was all muscle and weight, she was light, you know? Light and graceful.

We were such friends, Dana and me. When did I start to forget her? You've brought it all back, Cat. You, and the house going up for sale—and Jack.

86

***

Hi, Jack. Didn't expect to hear from you so soon….Yeah, the sign's still out there….Online? Sure, of course. I forget you can do that now….Well, I wouldn't know. I was never over there after you sold it….Day after tomorrow?…Are you?…Well, I'm at physio. Same place….If you want. There's a café just down the street. Just about where we bumped into each other, actually….Fine, we can talk more then.

You know, Cat, I haven't talked to him in what, 20 years maybe? That's the third call in three days, and now he wants to meet for coffee. I guess it's the house going up for sale.

He was heartbroken when Dana left him. I used to go over sometimes. She didn't have any friends or family, he said. No one else he could talk to about her but me. Grief had made him gentle, and the way he spoke…well, I believed he really loved her. It made me regret all the times I'd thought badly of him.

We'd been secret friends, Dana and me. She didn't have to tell me. It was the way she came over only when he wasn't there, and never called or invited me to join them or anything. Jack had a temper—I knew that from work. And there was something else about him, you know? Charming as all get out, but there was something you couldn't quite put your finger on that made you want to leave the room.

Oh, he was grief-stricken when she left him. And then he wasn't, had no interest in talking about her anymore. So in the end, it was a relief when he sold the place and moved on. A relief that he moved on, that is. Him selling, well, that just meant it was his to sell, you know? Which meant someone, somewhere, decided Dana was dead.

***

Hello again, Jack. I'm sorry you had to cancel, but you must've seen it online anyway....Just sold yesterday....I wouldn't know. It's bound to be a developer. No one buys these houses and leaves them alone....Well, maybe you could look that up. I won't know until the crew shows up to tear it down....Yes. Do. When you have more time.

***

You've found a nice spot for yourself there on the windowsill, Cat. You can still watch everything over there without getting wet.

It was raining that day, too—hard. I remember because the police officer wouldn't come right into the house. He just stood in the hall asking his questions, water dripping from his hat onto his notepad.

Jack had suddenly decided to report her missing. Told the police she must have been kidnapped or something. I was so shocked I thought I was going to pass out. I'd been so sure, you know, that she'd just packed up and gone.

All those mornings, sitting here and drinking tea. Dana knew about all these things that I didn't. About books, music. I started going back to the library, brought out the old tape deck. We sat on this couch and talked about everything. Well, everything outside of these houses, this street. We were going to travel one day—to New York, to London, see all the plays, the concerts. I could see the point of that now. We didn't talk about the lives we had, but rather the ones we were going to have. We were going to start over, Dana and me. We were going to be free.

I don't think the police took it seriously at first. They interviewed me, some of the other neighbors, I think. It was briefly on the news. A local mystery. I told them I didn't believe it. Said Jack just couldn't accept the fact that she would leave him. But time passed, and there was no word. People don't just disappear, they said. There's always a trail, but in this case there wasn't one.

I remember the day I saw the police car pull up to their garage doors. This was months after she went missing. It was the last time I thought she might be alive. I ran outside. I couldn't stop myself. They were standing there, leaning into each other the way people do when they're having a private chat. A comfortable little group, looking like they were just passing the time of day. I knew as soon as I saw them. They hadn't found her, and they weren't looking for her anymore.

And then I heard *him* laugh.

***

Hello again, Jack....Yes, the whole crew arrived yesterday. Couldn't start because of the rain. Came over to tell me the hydro was going down, so I asked them for you. Full basement, three storeys and a loft....Yes, a monster for sure....Oh....Hmm. I really don't have the time....I know. It's not that I—...All right....Yes....We can talk again later in the week then, can't we?

***

Did I slam down the phone, Cat? I felt like slamming down the phone. He keeps calling and then doesn't have time to talk, wants to meet and then doesn't show. If he wants to know about the house, why doesn't he just phone them and ask?

The whole thing is ridiculous. All these calls, turning on the charm, pumping me for information I obviously don't have. He could just get in the car and drive over here, for that matter. See for himself.

All this fuss about a house he sold 20 years ago. A house that belonged to Dana. And he hasn't even mentioned her name.

I never forgot the way he laughed that day. I didn't want to know him after that.

***

There was this one morning. It was winter, and Dana had made cinnamon buns; and the scent of cinnamon seemed to warm the house.

I could see she wasn't herself. It was in her eyes, in the way she moved. She was talking about how she wanted to see the River Thames in England. There were boats you could take, she said. You could sail all the way through London. But it was like she was just quoting lines from a book. Like she didn't believe in it anymore. Like she knew that these things were never actually going to happen.

We were back in the kitchen doing the dishes. She took her ring off, and it slipped and rolled across the floor. I picked it up for her. It was inscribed— tiny, tiny print but you could read it. Till Death Us Do Part, it said. I'd never thought Jack could be so romantic. He didn't seem the type at all.

I held it out to her, and for a moment I thought she wasn't going to take it. She just stood there, looking at it, as if she didn't know what it was.

***

Hello?...Jack. So you're back in town....Really. I see....No, just rather tired this....No, it seems this rain is never going to let up....Umm, it's a bit of a busy week for me so I'd—...Just for old times' sake....All right....Yes, call back later, when you have the date.

***

Cat, just look at you—wet and muddy and hungry. It isn't safe over there now. It really isn't. Come on in. I'll dry you off, if you'll let me, and feed you. I put a cushion on the chair by the window. The sill's rather a cold spot to stretch out on, don't you think?

There's something off about him. Something wrong. Ask me, though, and I wouldn't be able to tell you what it is. And the way he keeps calling. With nothing to say.

All these years, and I haven't thought about her. Not till you showed up. And what are you doing over there, Cat? What makes you sit there day after day, even now, when they're starting to pull it down?

Oh, I'm glad to see that house go, to tell you the truth. Dana's house. It's been a very long time. We were only friends for what? Two—no, three—years. Three years of secret friendship, cups of tea and dreaming of better things. I'd started to believe in it, you know? I'd started to believe I could get out of here, do something with my life. She gave me confidence, and she gave me hope. Then she was gone.

***

Hello? Jack....No actually, it isn't....I have no idea. There's some kind of delay, obviously....Hmm....Coming back again so soon? Really....Ah....Perhaps. I'll be there for an appointment....Yes, all right.... No. They'll just call me a cab.

***

I thought she'd walked away. And who would have blamed her? Stuck in that house, day after day, night after night, with *him*.

And this was a depressing place to live back then, believe me. Even when I was a kid, I knew it was a depressing place. The smell from that factory you wouldn't believe. No trees, no gardens even. And the noise, the constant hum behind everything. Only quiet on Sundays, when they had to close down.

I thought she would've told me, though. I thought she would've found a way to say good-bye before she left, or called, or written a letter. I thought we'd be friends forever.

To tell you the truth, when Jack reported her missing, I'd hoped it was true. It hurt less. It hurt less thinking she hadn't intended to stay away. More than that, it meant, of course, that she might come back. And I held on to that until that day the police pulled up to the house and I ran outside because I couldn't stop myself, and I heard him laugh.

***

Hello….Jack. I really don't feel like—…No, I understand you didn't but this is—….It has been quite the day, so if you don't mind I'd—…No….I understand…. Yes….I really have to go. Now.

***

Cats move their kittens when they don't feel safe. Where have you been? It isn't safe for you here anymore.

He drove right into me. I was just getting out of the cab. He almost ran over me, then turned on the charm. I'd forgotten just how charming he could be. Made such a fuss he had everyone thinking he was some kind of relation. I wasn't hurt, I said, just shaken, and I was going to physio anyway.

I had to insist he let me go so I could get there, and didn't he turn up in the waiting room ready to drive me home? I made them call me a cab, right then and there. Couldn't they see what he was doing? Couldn't they feel it?

What if he saw you, the doppelgänger, sitting out there the way you do?

And look at this. He was here, Cat. He must've been. This is her ring. This was outside my door this morning. He must've come right up to my door last night and put it there. Till Death Us Do Part. Dana wasn't kidnapped, and she never just walked away. I'm closing the curtains and locking you in, and then I'm taking it to the police. What did he think I was going to do with it?

***

Hello?...Jack....Did they?...No, I certainly wouldn't report you....Well, it wasn't me, so—...Jack, I really don't know what— ...It doesn't have anything to do with me....But the house is coming down, Jack, so I don't see—...Yes....A very long time ago, yes....Plea—...No, I won't be at home....I have no intent—...No, I said. No!

***

If he comes over, Cat, you must just disappear, okay? Don't go to the window. He mustn't see you.

He's there right now. Standing on the front steps. No police anywhere.

I should've known they wouldn't believe me. That detective—I could see the corners of his mouth twitching. Wish I could've talked to a woman.

If he comes over, you have to disappear. No matter what happens. Do you understand?

***

Hello?...Yes....He did?...Finally....He's gone already, then....How long?....Yes....Of course. Thank you, Officer, for letting me know....Yes, it's a relief, an immense relief.

***

I still don't understand how you got into that house, Cat, or how you got out, come to think of it. All the noise and commotion over there. You must have been so frightened.

You're looking much more settled now. Taken full possession of the chair. I hope you'll eventually make it onto my lap. You disappeared, then you came back.

The police said he was screaming something about a cat when they got there. Terrified, they said. He confessed, right there in the wreckage of your house. It's been quite the scene—fire department, police cars, forensic units, reporters.

And they found her. Finally, Cat, they found her.

The police told me something else, too. They said Jack told them he didn't leave that ring outside my door. He never had it. They showed it to him during the interview. The detective said she'd never seen anyone actually turn pale before, but he did. She has no idea how it got to my door.

It was you, Cat, wasn't it? It's been you all along. I don't know how it was you came to guard that house but it was you who started everything. I would've talked to Jack, maybe met him for coffee. The house would've been sold and torn down. When they started to dig, they might even have found her, but I wouldn't have known. He would've been long gone by then.

She was my first love, cat. I only just understood that. And I've been waiting for her—without even knowing I was waiting—for all these years.

Isn't it strange looking out the window and there's nothing there? There will be, of course. Eventually. I suppose, in situations like this, they have to wait until people forget.

You don't seem much interested in going out anymore. Are you planning on staying? I'd like it if you did. To be honest, I've grown rather attached to you, doppelgänger or not.

I should warn you, though, that I've been thinking about making a move. Not right away, but soon. Probably far from here.

I'm thinking it's time to start dreaming again. I'm thinking it's time to start over. A new beginning, Cat. For both of us.

About Rosalind Place

Rosalind Place was born in England and emigrated to Canada when she was five years old.

An interpreter by profession, she is a published writer of short stories and has just completed her first novel. "Dana's Cat", which is written entirely in dialogue, is her first foray into the mystery genre and she is thrilled that it was one of the stories chosen by the Mesdames to be part of *13 Claws*.

BLOOD AND APRICOTS

By Lisa de Nikolits

"What do you think happened?" my mother asked in a low voice.

She pressed the lighter into the dashboard, waited for a few seconds, lit a cigarette and passed it to my father. Then she lit one for herself and inhaled deeply.

We were driving on a highway. The mustard-colored lights cast a yellow spotlight on us, then faded. I could count the pauses. Yellow…fade to dark…yellow…fade to dark.

"His breath stinks," I said, shifting away from the dog who was sharing the backseat of the Volkswagen Beetle with me and my sister.

My sister put her arm around the dog. "I love him." She drew him closer, and I moved as far away from both of them as I could.

My father looked grim. The skin across his beautiful hands was stretched tight, and he gripped the steering wheel as if it might get away from him. He didn't say anything, just smoked now and then.

My mother looked out the window, to her left, and I saw the cameo outline of her profile, the profile that my face echoed.

I also wanted to know what had happened, but I knew my father would never answer if I asked, so I bit down my impatience and hoped my mother would ask again.

And she did, raising her voice. "What do you think happened?"

Once again, my father did not answer.

I went over what I knew.

We had gone over to my father's parents' place for Sunday night supper, as we always did. This generally made my mother jumpy and short-tempered. She and my *nagypapa*, my Hungarian grandfather, tolerated one another but no more than that. I didn't like him much, either. Once, he told me to say *pickle* in Hungarian or I wouldn't get one. I said, "So don't give me anything. See if I care." My father admonished me, but I knew he understood my side of things.

My grandmother, my *nagymama*, was an angel, quiet and kind. I kept close to her and ate two helpings of her food. I knew that she would love me, no matter what I did or didn't do in life.

When we arrived for supper that night, things were as they generally were. My *nagymama* was in the kitchen, preparing elaborate Hungarian dishes. My *nagypapa* was in his study, where my father went to join him; while my mother, my sister and I went out to the back patio.

I hauled myself up into a basket chair that hung from a thick steel chain, attached to a wooden panel on the ceiling. Part of me wanted that chair to come crashing down. "You see," I would say, "I knew the wooden beam couldn't hold it." But it did not crash, at least not that day, and I just swung back and forth.

My sister sat on the slate steps and examined her fingernails. I never knew anyone for examining their fingernails like my sister. What mystery they held, I could never fathom. My mother smoked and stared at nothing. I heard the sounds of my *nagymama* cooking—the scraping of a pan, the tapping of a wooden spoon on the side of a bowl, the running of water.

I knew my father would join us before too long because neither he nor my *nagypapa* could stand to be near each other for more than a few minutes. I was right; he soon appeared, and my mother wordlessly handed him the pack of cigarettes.

I looked across at the high wooden fence that circled the patio, and wondered if the garage was open. I had been warned against exploring the contents because I invariably got myself into trouble. But the place was so tempting; it was filled with trunks, chairs, lamps and bookcases, and I pretended to be a mountain climber, making my way to the topmost heap.

In Hungary, my *nagypapa* had been a judge, a wealthy man of noble blood with a family crest. I often wondered about the mansion he had left behind and hoped to rebuild one day. When the war broke out, he and my grandmother fled to South Africa with nothing but a small suitcase. He had forged a new life as a picture framer and a man who helped Jewish refugees.

The furniture in the garage was all polished wood, in light and dark shades. I had heard my father talk about a particular cabinet, calling it Birdseye Maple. I said the words to myself as I climbed my Everest stack: Birdseye Maple, Birdseye Maple. And then I tipped over, upside down. I swung there for hours, silent, wondering if anybody would find me.

They did, eventually, and my father told me not to go into the garage anymore. I had nodded but now, swinging in the basket chair, I looked over at the fence, at the very high, very dark fence that separated me from the stacks of polished wood.

I wondered how *nagypapa* could afford the collection in the garage, but I guessed he had accumulated it slowly, piece by painstaking piece.

It was so clean in the garage. I thought that my *nagypapa* must go in often and dust and polish his stockpile of treasures. He stockpiled all kinds of things—canned chestnut purée, canned cabbage with turkey, bottles of pitted sour cherries. The shelves of his tiny pantry were stacked three layers deep with cans that, unlike the other goods in the garage, were dusty, not polished and clean.

The pantry was filled with salami and spices, and to this day, when I go into an Eastern European store, I am transported back to when I was a child. I wondered at my grandfather's need for so much stored food. But I didn't understand then, not the way I do now.

I slipped out of the basket chair. "I am going to the orchard," I said, and my sister sat up and stopped looking at her fingernails. My mother and father were engaged in a quiet conversation, and I was sure it was about the money we didn't have—money for rent, school fees, and petrol and food and the like. I darted off to the orchard, ignoring my sister, who followed me like a swift ghost.

"It's all rotten here," I said to my sister, who was taken aback. And it was true, I never spoke to her if I could help it. I hadn't meant to talk to her; I was just saying what I thought out loud by mistake.

She leaned down and picked up an apricot. "*Nagypapa* should collect these before they fall," she said. "He lets them go to waste. He doesn't let anything else go to waste. He must hate apricots."

She sniffed the air. "It all smells of rotting apricots." She was right.

"I want to go into the garage," I said.

She shook her head. "You're not allowed."

But I led the way and she followed. The garage was next to the servants' quarters, which was home to a man we rarely saw—he cleaned the swimming pool and mowed the lawn. He was thin and old—at least, he was to me.

I had seen his wife once. She was round and timid and wore the maid's uniform of the day—a bleached, starched cotton dress, and a turban tightly wound around her head.

The garage door was unlocked, and I pulled it open. Later in life, antique stores would hit me with that same smell, ancient lives seeped into old wood, furniture that had absorbed the trials of endless days of trying to survive.

My sister sat down on the floor and examined her nails, while I clambered up onto a dining room table and mapped out my next ascent.

When my father came to find us for dinner, he seemed distracted and startled. And then he led us around the front of the house, not back through the orchard. I only thought about it in a vague way, like one of those things you don't really think about until later. Then you realize that you had missed the clues, including the ones that had been staring you in the face.

My father didn't join us for supper that night, and neither did my *nagypapa*. The police came, and they huddled around the servants' quarters. I could sense all kinds of activity outside, but I wasn't allowed to look or ask questions. My mother and my *nagymama* were silent. We picked at our food. I could tell my mother wanted to go out to smoke, but she wasn't allowed outside, either.

And then we went home. Only now we had a dog with us. A big black Labrador with terrible breath and a thick coat that needed a bath. He was an old dog, with white around his muzzle. His eyebrows were gray, and so was some of the hair on his paws.

"The blood was coming out from under the door," my father finally said. He leaned back in his seat as if trying to push himself away from the memory of what he had seen.

"His wife?" my mother asked. I knew she was trying to say as little as possible in front of us although my sister wasn't listening.

My father nodded. "So much blood," he said. "And he was in the corner of the room, with his back to all of it, and the dog next to him. I would never have known, if I hadn't seen the blood spilling out like that. And if I had come by a few minutes earlier, I would never have seen it."

"But your father would have, the next day."

My father shrugged. "Maybe. It was too late anyway. He'll go to jail. No one even knew his wife was still there. We thought she'd gone home. She had been sent home, that's what my parents thought. She wasn't needed, so they sent her home. She should have gone."

I wondered if the dog had got any blood on him. I tried to examine him in the spaces of yellow light, but they flashed by too quickly.

I tried to move even farther away from him, but then I held out my hand and touched his rough, bear-like hide. He seemed exotic now, filled with secrets I could never know. He knew how a man could kill his wife, cut her up so badly that her blood would flow across the concrete floor and spill in a quiet lake down the steps outside the door.

"What shall we call him?" I asked my sister.

SNAKE OIL

By M.H. Callway

Young women marry money. Women of a certain age turn to real estate.

Mean words with an icy sliver of truth, Bella thought.

Beyond her BMW's cracked windshield, dry snow whirled down the empty residential street. Only one word could describe February in Toronto and that word was *bleak*.

She thumbed through her freshly printed business cards. Gilt-edged, copperplate writing. Old-fashioned but classy, because class was all she had left. She couldn't trump the swag that adorned the business cards of her young rival, John, with their QR codes and laser hologram logos that rotated and winked at you.

She hugged herself and breathed in and out in desperate self-affirmation.

I can do this. I know I can do this.

She'd taken a careful look-see drive down the street earlier. Maintenance of the houses so-so. Roof tiles crumbling on many, paint flaking off a few others. And not a single For Sale sign on the street. Not even one.

Hardly promising. Still, it was February and houses didn't sell in winter.

Maybe this street is a street of junk, she thought. The no-hopers that Wolfeband Realty dumped on its junior agents: the failed renovations, the hoarder palaces, the firetraps, the termite infestations, the abandoned grow-ops, the murder houses…

But there was one prize—the brick Victorian halfway down the north side of the street. Its large lot meant money. Maybe even big money. God, she'd give anything to get a peek inside.

One of Wolfeband's legendary business coups dealt with a neglected Riverdale mansion. When the new owners tore down its dingy ceiling tiles, they'd uncovered beautiful ornamental medallions and crown molding, all museum-perfect. HGTV had featured the historical home's restoration, with Wolfeband's perspicacity greatly credited.

I could pull that off, too. I've got an eye for quality. All I need is a chance.

But how to talk her way inside that brick Victorian? She hadn't a clue where to begin. She'd had no practice, because, damn it, Amelia hadn't given her a chance to sell *anything.*

Amelia. Brilliant top agent Amelia.

Wolfeband's Greatest Legend centred on a semidetached house where an elderly woman had been lying dead for a month. Amelia sold the corpse-free half of the semi after convincing her young buyers that the strange stink permeating their prospective home would dissipate once they installed a working sewer back-up. Hence the proffered 5% discount. The young couple took the bait and with it, Wolfeband's homegrown guarantee: You Bought It, You Got It.

Inevitably the dead body was discovered. Just as inevitably, the paramedics were wheeling it out on the day of closing. Even better at the exact moment when the new owners landed on their new front porch brandishing their shiny new house key. Did they flee in horror? No way: they moved in as planned. As first-time buyers, they didn't have a cent left over for a lawsuit.

But the *coup de grâce* came four days later when Amelia unloaded the tainted half of the semi. Admittedly at a deep discount, but a sale nonetheless. And those thrifty buyers also stayed put. Champagne all round!

And the overarching moral of this story? At Wolfeband Realty, business ethics was an oxymoron.

Okay, I can accept that. In fact, I'm more than fine with it, Bella thought. *So why the hell won't Amelia do what she's supposed to do as my mentor and help me?*

From the first day of her realtor internship, Bella couldn't get a read on Amelia. Couldn't connect with her. Hardly auspicious.

What more can I do? she thought. *Suck up even harder? Land cash-rich buyers and drop them at Amelia's feet like a good little kitty bringing home a dead mousie? She'll just swipe my commissions. I just know it. I can tell.*

Now that she'd turned off her aging BMW's engine to save gas, a chill had settled throughout its interior. The whine of the winter wind buffeting the sides of the sedan only intensified her sense of isolation.

There must be more money. There must be more money.

Lately that phrase from the D. H. Lawrence story, "The Rocking-Horse Winner," had surfaced from her teaching days and mutated into a stubborn brain worm. Her English students never appreciated the doom and inevitability of the tale. They considered the merciless exploitation of a small child by his greedy parents a trite, overdone scenario. She'd only succeeded in boring them, exactly as her ex, Barry, had predicted.

The way I bored him, too.

After Barry walked out, she'd sworn to keep her lifestyle. No way would she let that deserting rat destroy her.

But Barry didn't believe in alimony. How else could he afford three ex-wives and a grand lifestyle? Damn foolish to sign that prenup—what had she been thinking? But luckily her lawyer had managed to register their Moore Park home in both their names. Oh, Barry had argued and wrangled and shouted, but in the end, he gave in. His new fiancée was getting restless. Moore Park became hers, free and clear and rightfully so. She'd damn well earned it.

She redecorated at once to wipe away every trace of Barry. She continued to shop at Holt's and to party with her friends at the golf club. Life, at first, proved far more pleasant without Barry around, sulking and picking at her faults. But over time, the costs of running the Moore Park house ate through her investments like cancer. In the end, she'd been forced to unload everything and quickly, too. She'd had to quit the golf club, cut up her credit cards...

How quickly her friends had vanished! How fast she dwindled into an unhappy warning of what happened when a wealthy husband grew bored, or felt unfulfilled, or feared growing old...

There must be more money. There must be more money.

Strangely enough, her stepson, Robert, remained her ally. They met for coffee from time to time, usually at Balzac's in Union Station, before he caught the GO Train back home to his wife and kids in the suburbs.

"I'll never understand Dad," Robert confided. "I really had my hopes up for you two. You seemed so perfect together, I mean, you both loved golf and traveling. And third time lucky for Dad, right?"

"Second time for me," Bella put in. She'd settled for Martin rather than endure her 40s as a single woman. Poor Martin—boring, suburban, predictable, safe. The golf club had saved her. Hard work to land Martin's golf buddy, Barry. Harder work to pry him loose from Wife Number

Two and to persuade him to commit. But the hardest work of all had been trying to keep him happy. Ultimately the golf, bird-watching and world cruises had failed. Socializing with his contemporaries proved to be a constant, unpleasant reminder of his age.

"It's like the day he turned 65, he lost his mind," Robert said. "Number Four is 32! She's five years younger than me for God's sake!"

"And do you know what the old fool is up to now?" he went on. "He's doing the Dakar Rally from Bolivia to Argentina with that woman. On a two-seater motorbike. Insanity! He's going to get himself killed and her, too."

Good, Bella thought. *I hope he does die. I hope his motorbike crashes into a cliff and they burn alive. I hope the banditos ass-rape him and slit his throat. And they gang-rape her and cut her into little pieces while she's still alive.*

But Barry and Wife Number Four didn't die. Their motorbike broke down almost immediately and they were out of the race. No, Martin was the one who died in a single-car crash on the Gardiner Expressway. Suicide, the police hinted. She'd never learned for sure because Martin's family had cut her off. They even barred her from attending his funeral.

Some dark, lonely days, she wished she'd turned her pricey Henkel carving knife on Barry instead of attacking the Christmas turkey during their last epic fight. Raw flesh everywhere.

Not that Barry's deserving death would save her from her latest financial crisis. She hadn't told Robert the full story. Too embarrassing. When Barry finally married her, she'd quit teaching to live the lifestyle she deserved. At the time, the prospect of a seriously diminished pension seemed irrelevant. Chump change. But now, she couldn't even cover her rent, let alone her debts.

She let slip that she'd have to move again soon.

Robert threw her a look. "Bella, are you having money problems again? Look, I know it's been a while, but why don't you go back to teaching?"

No, you idiot, Bella wanted to shout. *The board would never hire me back. Too many years and too many burned bridges.*

Then her hairstylist described how her cousin had made a fortune in real estate. Sparked by desperation and vengeance, Bella seized on the idea. When she was forced to unload the Moore Park home, she'd been outfoxed, cajoled and finally bullied into a price well below its market value. Rearmed with knowledge, she could beat those real estate agent snakes at their own game. Recoup the money she'd lost, buy back her house!

"I don't know about you and real estate," Robert said after she outlined her plans. "You taught high school. You've never done sales."

But she passed the real estate board exam with flying colors.

"That's great, Bella. Brilliant," Robert said. "Go push condos for a developer. You'll earn a good salary, work regular hours—"

"I can't live on some pitiful salary," Bella cut him off. "I need to make decent money. That means high-end, exclusive properties. Only high-end."

"Okay, sure, but you'll be showing empty houses to people you know nothing about. Going into the homes of strangers. A woman, alone. Anything can happen. Take it from me, there are a lot of weirdos out there."

"Really, Robert, it's not like I'll be showing dumps. Weren't you listening? High-end properties, only high-end. That screens out the weirdos right there."

But life after Barry had a way of *not* working out. Any hope she'd had of hiring on at Wolfeband Realty after her internship had quickly evaporated. From the first day, Amelia anointed the other intern, John, as the Chosen One. No doubt because he was much younger and more stylish, as well as adept at technology that terrified or confused Bella. These days, the Chosen One talked over and around her as though she didn't exist, indifferent to the fact that she overheard everything he said.

Despite what he thought about her, if he thought about her at all, she wasn't stupid or oblivious. Yesterday she'd taken charge. Done what she should have done in the first place.

Drafts blew through the BMW. Bella flexed her gloved fingers to get the blood flowing. She studied her reflection in the driver's mirror and fluffed her short blond hair. Was that a glint of pink scalp? No, it was this strange daylight, it had to be. Her hair was not getting thin. She was simply being paranoid as Barry loved to tell her.

Though I guessed right about you and Number Four, she thought, and shivered. She hadn't dressed for the weather this morning, because she'd dressed for the part.

To make money in real estate, dress like you're rich already. Amelia's latest pearl of wisdom, hastily dropped. Her not-so-thinly veiled criticism had stung, though Bella conceded that her image needed some sprucing up. But how? She was buying groceries on her credit card for God's sake.

There must be more money. There must be more money.

Still, classic styles lasted forever, right? So last night, she'd hauled out her favorite coat from the back of the closet. Scarlet cashmere wool, full cut, with long, fringed front panels like scarves. To her horror, she spotted a moth casing on the floor right underneath it. Another moth casing fell out when she stripped off the plastic shroud of the dry cleaner's bag. Her frantic search uncovered two tiny holes on the inside sleeve.

And the drafty air inside the BMW couldn't hide the solvent smell of the black marker pen she'd used to paint out the scratches on her fancy ankle boots, scratches that shoe polish had failed to cover.

A sharp rap on the passenger window set Bella's heart racing. The door on the passenger side flew open in a blast of icy air. A flurry of white fur and cashmere as Amelia Greene settled down into the passenger seat.

"I thought I recognized your car." Amelia dropped her Versace bag on the floor and leaned back, balancing a Starbucks cup on her knee. "Are you all right? Did I scare you?"

Bella stared. For a moment, the pungent odor of Amelia's perfume and seared latte overwhelmed her.

"Earth to Bella," Amelia said. "How did it go at the doctor's this morning? Not bad news, I hope."

"No, no." Bella said, remembering her lie. "Everything's fine." She'd been so lost in thought that she hadn't heard Amelia's Mercedes pull up an inch behind her BMW.

Amelia rested her latte in Bella's coffee-stained cup holder and rummaged through her purse. "Here, these are for you." She held out a small, black cardboard box.

Bella took the box from her and opened it. Business cards, printed on heavy cream paper with a gilt edging. Embossed with Wolfeband's rotating hologram logo and, of course, Amelia's name.

"Is something wrong?"

"No, absolutely not." Bella rammed the lid back on the box and set it on the dash.

"Good, good." Amelia's lacquered red nails tapped the BMW's sun-bleached dashboard next to the box. "Tell me, what's your take on this street?"

Bella cleared her throat. "Judging by the cars in the driveways, middle-class. No For Sale signs, so settled, low turnover."

"And the next step?"

"Check out the homes that need repairs or look vacant."

"Which means?"

"A quick and dirty estate sale. Sales price takes a hit, but the family will want to unload it and fast."

"So you have been listening to me after all." Amelia took a thoughtful sip of latte. "Okay, instead of coming in to the office this afternoon, why don't you take my business cards and work the street. Knock on doors, chat them up. And shove a card in the mail box if no one's at home."

Bitch! Bella thought. "Amelia, we need to talk."

"All right." Amelia's onyx eyes widened slightly. "What's on your mind?"

There must be more money. There must be more money.

"Knocking on doors, dropping off your business cards, well, I'm not sure that's the best use of my time right now." There, she'd stood up for herself at last.

"Actually, it's the best possible use of your time."

"I've got to start earning money. I can't go on working for free any longer."

Amelia leaned back, latte in hand. "This is an internship, Bella. No guarantee of income. You knew that when you signed on at Wolfeband."

"But John started when I did. I know for a fact that you gave him that new condo development on Eglinton. He bagged two sales yesterday. He told me so himself." She tried to read Amelia's pale, perfect features, but couldn't.

"I don't want to be unkind," Amelia said at last. "But that new condo is aimed at buyers under 40. John's young, vibrant. Buyers relate to him."

"But not to me."

"I see you working a suburban market."

The suburbs? "I'm better than that," Bella muttered.

Annoyance flashed across Amelia's face. "Bella, real estate isn't easy money, despite what your friends may have told you. You have to beat the bushes for buyers, give up your weekends to run open houses, read the biz papers to spot trends, build your network. That's hours and hours of work that won't pay you a dime. The only time you make money is when you close a sale. Listen carefully. *Close* a sale."

"Yes, overcoming buyer objections." John loved to brag about his priceless skill at overcoming objections.

"Of course, that goes without saying. But to close a sale, your buyer has to be begging to sign that offer. You've got to get them hungry." Amelia's onyx eyes flared with a gold glint. "Then you go in for the kill."

What crap, Bella thought.

"Tell me, why *did* you choose real estate?" Amelia took a long, luxurious swallow of her latte. "Nothing personal, but I'm not sure why you chose this business."

"What do you mean?" Bella's skin prickled, as though she'd been attacked by a thousand little needles. Was that why Amelia had pulled over to chat? Much easier to fire her out of the office. Drama and histrionics relegated off-stage.

"I don't sense that killer sales instinct in you. Come on, don't look so upset. Better you hear this now, from me, before you invest more time and effort and end up frustrated and disappointed." Amelia wiped a thin froth of latte from her upper lip. "Still, to be fair, I do sense something in you, a certain doggedness perhaps. Let's try to build on that."

Now what? Threat, then carrot? Bella gripped the steering wheel to stop her fingers from squeezing the life out of Amelia's soft white throat.

"Okay, I should get going." Amelia leaned forward to check her reflection in the rear-view mirror. With her little finger, she smoothed her scarlet lipstick and as she did so, her white fur cuff fell back with a flash of light.

Gold scales, ruby eyes. Bella let out a gasp of horror. "Your-your…bracelet."

"What? This?" Amelia held up her arm. A golden snake curled around her smooth wrist, the reptile's fangs biting its tail. "He's my good luck piece. My snake oil, if you will."

"I…I hate snakes."

Amelia's glossy red lips curved into a smile. She slid the fur cuff back over her wrist, hiding the bracelet. "There. Better now?"

"I—I was bitten by a snake." Bella could barely get the words out. The memory charged at her in irregular flashes, like crumpled black-and-white photographs. "I was walking on the beach by our cottage. I felt something sharp. Like I'd stepped on a piece of glass."

She felt Amelia's slanted eyes on her like a pressure. She must stop talking, she was being horribly unprofessional, but she couldn't stop the eruption of her words any more than she could stop the winter wind pummeling her car. "Robert, my stepson, wanted to take me to the hospital. Barry, my ex, thought…it was nothing. That I was overreacting. He said I'd stepped on a garter snake, but when it…when it rustled away in the leaves, it looked much bigger. And it had black spots, not stripes."

"But you're still here, Bella, alive and healthy."

Bella's words stormed out with the rush of remembering. "My leg swelled up. The pain was excruciating. Robert took me to the hospital. Barry wouldn't...he didn't believe me." She took a deep, shuddering breath. "I'd stepped on a Massasauga rattler. The doctors had to inject me with antivenom. They had a hard time finding enough of the antidote, because poisonous snake bites are so rare in Ontario. Antivenom goes off if it's stored too long. I—I nearly lost my leg."

"Sounds like your divorce was a good idea," Amelia said after a time. "Feel better for sharing?"

"Yeah, I guess." Bella wiped her eyes.

"Good. Now back to business. Tell me, of all the houses on the street, which one gives you the kick? Which one feels better than sex? Which one would you just kill to sell?"

Yet another test. Bella knew which house all right, but why bolster Amelia's puffed-up ego? In spite of herself, her eyes drifted to the large, red brick Victorian halfway up the street.

"*Very* good." Amelia flashed a smile. "That one *is* a challenge. Okay, let's see what you can do with it. Off you go. I need to get back to the office." She dropped her empty Starbucks container in Bella's cup holder and gathered up her purse to leave.

Finally! About time you fucked off, Bella thought.

"Don't forget these." Amelia tapped the black box of business cards Bella had left on the dash.

Like hell, Bella thought, gripping her own business cards in her coat pocket. *This one's mine.*

***

The raw wind tossed the fringes on Bella's red coat and raked through her hair. Her scalp and ears were throbbing with cold by the time she'd crossed over the

114

snow-dusted street. The sidewalk was crusted with ice and slippery as the devil. She teetered along on her spike-heeled ankle boots, balancing her handbag on her shoulder as she made for her Victorian prize.

Amelia's AMG Mercedes roared to life behind her and took off down the street. For a moment, she felt utterly abandoned. Not a soul in sight. No letter carrier, no repair person, no one at all.

The houses lining the street now struck her as tawdry. The Victorian, too, proved to be a letdown as she approached it. The footpath leading to its porch wasn't stone or brick, but stained concrete with long tufts of dried grass poking through the weathered cracks. Half of the front yard was snow-strewn gravel, probably a parking pad, while the other half was covered in scraggly weeds, yellow islets marooned in a shifting sea of dry snow.

No car on the parking pad. What if Amelia knew that no one was at home this time of day? What if Amelia had set her up?

Only one way to find out. Bella stumbled up the ice-slick stairs of the verandah. Someone in their non-wisdom had painted its railings, balustrade and support columns a matte black color, but the paint was flaking off, revealing a bone-white undercoat. The large windows on either side of the front door were sealed with metal foil. Impossible to see inside. Through the transom window over the door, she noticed that the hall light was on. The light fixture wasn't elegant, but a functional white globe left over from the 1960s.

She flicked the edges of her business cards in her coat pocket.

I can do this. I know I can do this.

The doorbell was a rectangular press button set in a yellowing plastic frame. She pressed it and listened.

A scuffling noise behind the front door. For a moment, she had the eerie sensation of being watched, though she couldn't spot a peephole in the door.

The scuffling stopped, but the door didn't open. Her legs stung with cold. She'd turned to leave, when she heard the click of a lock behind her.

The door opened. Warm humid air rushed out.

"Um, hi!" she began.

A tall, thin man wearing a black T-shirt and worn jeans looked out at her. His arms were ropy with muscle, his long hair gray and unkempt. She guessed his age to be about 50, far younger than the senior citizen she'd expected. Despite the cold, he was barefoot: his elongated, pale toes bony, their opaque nails edged with black dirt.

"Can I help you with something?" he asked.

She had her business card out. "I'm Bella Bates of Wolfeband Realty. I was passing by your neighborhood today and I was wondering, um, I was curious to know if, well, you were thinking of putting your home on the market in the near future."

Whew, that was a mouthful, she thought.

"I might be." He accepted her card, held it by the edges. "Would you like to come in?"

"What, um, oh, yes, thanks." She hesitated on the threshold. The front hall looked small and cramped, not inviting at all.

She'd expected the house to be a centre hall plan with a broad central staircase leading to the upper floors. Perhaps a wood-paneled library to her left, a parlor and dining room to her right. But instead, the hallway was divided in two by a blank sheet of white. Wallboard, she realized, reaching out her left hand to touch it. And to her right, she saw a heavy brown curtain, hiding the main room beyond it from view.

No sign of the staircase to the upper levels. Judging by the short length of the entrance hall, someone had blocked it off with more sheets of faceless wallboard.

A slithering sound: the man brushed back the curtain. He motioned her through the dark gap. She hesitated, then chided herself for being foolish. Here was her chance to see the house. She'd fought for this. What could possibly happen?

I can do this. I know I can do this.

She stepped past the curtain into the dark of the main room.

Her first impression was one of deep disappointment. She'd been hoping for, praying for rare beauty, an HGTV showpiece. Not that John, the Chosen One, shared her love of Victoriana and Art Deco. He raved about today's stark, disposable interiors, as bleak and as interchangeable as a dentist's office. How he would have loved this place.

The long, rectangular room was almost devoid of furniture, its white-painted walls entirely bare. Long ago, someone had shrouded its floor in beige linoleum, but over time the lino had worn away into layered islands and peninsulas over a sea of naked subflooring that felt gritty underfoot. Antique cast-iron radiators leaned against the walls like random sculptures. The ceiling soared 10 feet above her head. Two antique light fixtures, 1930s she supposed, cast down an anemic light. Their red, faux marble bowls were festooned with cobwebs and encrusted with insect life.

A long, battered table stretched across the far end of the room. Its surface was buried in papers, disposable dishes and cups, and what appeared to be a number of empty aquariums. A laptop stood open, lights blinking.

A hard-backed wooden chair leaned against one end of the table. The only other furniture, two antique plywood chairs, the kind she'd last seen in high school, stood in the centre of the room facing the table like audience seating before a stage.

"Please, sit down." He indicated one of the two side-by-side plywood chairs. He took the chair at the table and turned on the steel desk lamp resting on it. Its light pierced her eyes. She felt like a prisoner about to be interrogated.

"So," he said, studying her business card, "you said you're with Wolfeband Realty. It doesn't say so on here."

"No, I've just started with them. I may not stay on. I haven't decided." She felt herself babbling. "You know how it is."

"Of course."

"Have you—have you lived here long? In this house, I mean."

"Long enough." He smiled with a hint of yellowish teeth. "What would you like to know?"

What wouldn't I like to know? Bella thought. "Well, um, let's start with the basics. How many rooms do you have?"

"I really don't know."

"Um, what?"

He shrugged. "I don't live in most of the house."

"Oh, but...how long did you say you've lived here?"

"I didn't say." He thought for a moment, his brows knitting together. "April, 1996. But you could look that up at City Hall, couldn't you?"

"Yes, of course." Twenty years! He'd lived here for 20 years! But surely not like this, like a destitute student. Where did he sleep? Cook food? Shower? The way some people lived never ceased to amaze her.

Perhaps, like herself, he was a casualty of divorce. Perhaps to keep the house, he'd been forced to shed all his worldly possessions. She could relate to that.

Now what? He seemed at ease sitting there, legs crossed, not saying a damn thing. All right, she'd work to engage him. Discover his innermost desires, his dreams. What Amelia did as naturally as breathing.

He wasn't the type of man she normally encountered. The two dates she'd landed through that Internet dating site were sixtyish, wrapped in soft fat and self-satisfaction. They'd expected sex right away, as though they were granting *her* a lovely favor. Horrible!

This man looked hungry, too, but in a different way. His thinness extended to his face, the hollows and creases deep, the bones prominent. His eyes seemed strange. What was it, their peculiar yellow-gray color? No, it was the iris of his left eye. It looked torn as though his dark pupil was bleeding across it.

No doubt he was waiting her out, to compel her to speak first. He probably had lots of realtors salivating over his large property. He probably loved baiting them.

"Your house is interesting," she lied. "Can you tell me when was it built?"

"I have no idea. And to be honest, I don't find this house particularly interesting."

Damn! Amelia never asked direct questions. She always posed open-ended, soft questions. A *what* question. Get *them* to talk.

"What do you know about its history?"

"History?" His brow wrinkled, and she realized another unsettling thing about his face. He had no eyebrows at all. "Why would you want to know that?"

"Um, well, if you had some interesting anecdotes about this house, buyers might find them entertaining. Enticing."

"Enticing?" His lips twitched. "Well, the guy over the back fence claims they ran a store in here back in the 1950s.

When he was a kid, he'd come over to buy candy. Jawbreakers."

Oh, yes, the candy that turned from black to red as you sucked on it, staining your tongue and teeth black and red, too. She forced a smile. "That's exactly the kind of story I'm looking for. Anything else?"

"Some frat guys got drunk and painted the outside bricks pink."

"This was a frat house?" Come to think of it, the street did run close to the university, which would explain why houses looked so battered and run-down. Student housing. "Obviously you had it painted back to a normal color. To a brick color, I mean."

"Obviously."

Painted brick could be a problem, she thought. The house couldn't breathe. Humidity, mildew, you name it.

In fact, she felt hot and sticky enough to unbutton her coat. She retrieved a tissue from her handbag and wiped her forehead.

"Hot flash?" He looked amused.

"Excuse me?"

"You're sweating."

"It is rather warm in here." The inside windows were running with moisture. Water dripped down the panes, etching dark lines of mildew along the wooden frames. Paint chips littered the window sashes and the floor beneath them like snow.

Maybe he liked to crank up the heat to pretend he was barefoot on a beach, she thought. Cheaper and safer than traveling to Mexico.

Her eyes wandered over the walls, the baseboards, the ceiling, searching for anything she might coax back to beauty.

No, the room was too empty. More than empty—lifeless.

Perhaps that bleak wallboard dividing the hall hid marvels waiting to be uncovered in the other half of the house, but judging by what she'd seen so far, that seemed unlikely. To sell the house, she'd have to play up its interior as an empty canvas.

But what about that odor? Barry, her ex, always accused her of snuffling, of being overly fussy and fastidious. But this smell couldn't be ignored. She felt an urgency to define it. Earthy? Damp? It didn't belong in a house, nor would she associate it with a garden. What if it was a sewer backup?

"You're staring," he said.

"I'm studying this room, visualizing the before and after," she improvised. "I love doing that with every home I visit. I feel like I'm healing it, bringing it back to life. Not the way it actually was before, you know, undiscovered and unappreciated, but the way it should have been."

"Is that how you feel? That you're undiscovered and unappreciated?"

"What?" For a moment she wasn't sure that she'd heard him correctly. She forced out a laugh. "That's rather personal."

He smiled and waved a hand. "Carry on with your visualizing. Don't let me stop you."

She mustered her thoughts. "What I meant to say, what I'm suggesting, is that a few enhancements could really up the sales price of your home. This room could be stunning if you put up high-quality chandeliers, wainscoting on the walls and crown molding round the ceiling. At the very least, you need to install baseboards round the floor."

He made an impatient gesture. "I ripped all that junk out."

"What? You did what?"

"Ornate busywork. Unnecessary and confusing to the mind."

"That's a strange, I mean, unusual way of looking at things. I…" At the edge of her peripheral vision, something moved. A dark form like a tail vanished into the shadows under the nearby radiator. She stared, not sure what she had seen. *If* she had seen it.

She stood up. "Something's under that rad."

He lifted one shoulder, unperturbed.

"Right over there." She pointed. "I saw it. You don't have rats, do you?"

He laughed, he actually laughed. "No, Bella Bates, we don't have rats. Rats wouldn't survive long in here."

"I definitely saw something." But what? In the murky, diffuse light of the room, how could she be sure? And unless she crouched down beside the radiator for a closer look, stuck her hand into the dark underneath…

She gripped the back of the chair.

"Would you like to look around?" he asked.

She opened her mouth to say no, that she'd seen enough, that she needed to get back to the office. But that would be giving in. Amelia would win. John, the Chosen One, would sell it out from under her.

I can do this. I know I can do this.

"Still deciding?" he asked.

She straightened up. "Of course, yes, thank you. I do need to do a thorough look around." She set down her purse and groped through it for her notebook and pen.

"I thought all you real estate types used a tablet," he said.

"No, I'm old-school." She clutched her notebook to her chest, determined to project cheerful efficiency.

"You'll want to see the kitchen."

"Yes, the kitchen and the bathroom. But I'd like to look upstairs first." She was determined to see what lay behind that wallboard in the hall.

"We don't use the upper floor. I walled it off."

"Whatever for?"

"To seal in the heat."

But it feels like 40 degrees in here, you fool, she thought. She'd been so chilled from sitting outside in the car that at first, the stinking, tropical heat hadn't bothered her. But now sweat leaked from her armpits and trickled down her back. She longed to shed her coat, but instinct urged her to keep it on.

She wiped her forehead with the crumpled tissue, knowing she'd missed something. Yes! He'd said *we* not *I*. He'd said, "*We* don't use the upper floor." She tried to spot signs of the other person, but saw nothing.

"Do you have a tenant?" she asked.

"Why do you ask?"

"Well, if I understand you correctly, you've walled off half of your ground floor and all of your upstairs. Like a makeshift semi." When he shrugged, she went on, "That's vacant space, an underutilized asset. You should to put it to work for you, earn you some money."

"I don't think more people in this house would a good idea. Shall we?" He gestured toward the arched doorway at the far end of the room beyond the table.

All Bella could see as she passed the table was yet another bare façade of wall board beyond the archway. Where was the hall that led to the rooms at the back of the house?

"How exactly do you get through to the kitchen?" she asked.

"I'll show you. Go ahead." He waved her through the doorway.

She hesitated, notebook pressed to her chest, then eased closer to where he stood. In the dim light, she could make out a narrow passage to her right. A few feet along, it veered sharply left at a 90-degree angle, presumably continuing on to the kitchen at the back of the house. But why the wallboard? What feature of the house had he hidden this time?

"Don't you want to look at the kitchen?" he asked.

She shook her head and took a step back. That's when she spotted it: a steel door handle sticking out of the wallboard panel to her left. That must be the way into the unused half of the house. "Why don't I take a look in here first?"

She seized the handle. It turned easily enough, and a portion of the wallboard swung open like a door, revealing only dark beyond.

"Don't you have a light?" she asked.

He sighed audibly and reached through the doorway, pressing close to her as he did so. She could feel his sinewy body, breathe in his strange smell: part male sweat, part unwashed clothes...

The click of a switch. A faint light came on. She stepped free of him into the space beyond the door.

This room, too, was large, the mirror image of the one she'd left behind. Except its walls were lined with bookshelves. Row upon row upon row of books. Stacks of paper rested on the shelves or were stacked on the bare wooden floor.

"I don't understand," she said. "What is this place? A storeroom?"

He didn't reply, but even in the weak light, she caught his smirk of a smile.

Where was the staircase? She should have been standing immediately in front of it. "I don't see the stairs."

"I ripped them out."

"What? You did what?" By now her eyes had adjusted enough to the dimness that she could see a large hole in the ceiling, framed by a crumbling rim of plaster and broken subflooring. "But—but why?"

"They were falling apart. Haven't got round to rebuilding them yet."

"What if you need to go upstairs to check for leaks or wiring or…"

"I use a ladder when I have to go up. I'll set it up for you. Climb up, take a look round. Take as long as you want." He smiled again.

Her neck flared with electric warnings. Yes, she could climb up only to have him remove the ladder. She'd be trapped upstairs. No one knew where she was except Amelia. No one. And when she didn't turn up at the office, would Amelia look for her? Call the police? No, she'd assume that she, Bella, had quit real estate, exactly as predicted.

And Robert, her stepson? They only saw each other every few weeks.

I could lie there forever. No one would find me.

She managed a normal voice. "Sorry, I can't climb a ladder in these boots. I'll get the details from City Hall—as you suggested."

He filled the doorway, blocking her way back to the main room. A shuffling noise behind him startled her.

"What was that?" She heard breathing in the narrow hallway that led to the kitchen. The other person!

"Who is that?" she said more loudly. She groped for her handbag, then remembered she'd left it on the chair in the main room. Her cell phone was in it.

She heard something or someone scurry away. Something much larger than a mere rat. Heading toward the back of the house.

I have to get out of here!

No choice: she squeezed past the man and charged back into the main room. Her purse was gone.

"Where's my bag? Someone stole my bag."

He held up a hand. "No one's stolen anything."

"My wallet, keys and phone are in there."

"I'll look after it. Stay here." He ducked down the narrow passage, turned the corner and vanished toward the back of the house.

She waited and waited. Counted to 20, then 50. Where the hell was he?

Instinct urged her to get out. To go back to the office. Call the police. But everything was in her bag, including her car keys.

She took a step, hesitated. Forced herself to go after him. Felt her way down the narrow hall, turned the sharp corner. Watery daylight streamed through an open door at end of the hall.

She groped her way into a cramped, outdated kitchen. Her eyes took in aging appliances, battered cupboards and filthy countertops. The far end of the room gave onto dripping windows blank against the gray, snow-filled sky. No sign of the man.

Where was the back door, the way out? She moved closer to the windows. A shallow set of steel-edged stairs led down from the kitchen to a landing at ground level.

A shadowy figure hovered on the landing.

"Oh, my God!"

She had an impression of dark, straggling hair and hunched shoulders in a ragged hoodie. Abruptly the person vanished. Running footsteps: where did they go?

More footsteps! Her heart was beating so frantically, she wheezed for air. The gray-haired man appeared on the shallow steps leading up to the kitchen. He bounded up into the kitchen.

"There you go." He tossed her bag onto the counter top beside her, then busied himself at the sink on the opposite side of the room.

She grabbed her purse. "That—that person took it. Who is he?"

"Don't worry about him."

It's over. Let it go. She eased out a breath. Normal, she had to act normal. "So—so this is your kitchen."

"Obviously."

The cupboard doors bore so many coats of beige paint they looked enamelled. Dirty dishes and cooking pots crowded the counters. Strangely enough, a stainless steel Mixmaster and a set of top-of-the-line carving knives squatted among them. The knife stand was shaped like a man, the knife blades skewering him like a murder victim.

She'd bought the exact same set the day Barry signed their divorce papers.

The man was still busy at the sink. She shoved her notebook back into her bag and slipped over to the far end of the kitchen. One quick look out the windows at the back garden, then she'd be off.

The windows framed the back end of the kitchen on three sides. He must have knocked out the back wall separating the kitchen from the enclosed back porch, then put in the stairs down to the ground level.

Impossible to see through the watery mist covering the panes. She found the crumpled tissue in her coat pocket. Balancing at the top of the stairs, she leaned over, wiped off the window beside her and looked out.

Deep snow blanketed a wilderness of tangled weeds, tall enough to reach over her head. A 10-foot board fence stretched behind them. What would happen if she left through the back door? What if there was no gate out of the yard? She could almost feel the chill of snow on her thighs as she struggled through the straw of the dead plants, screaming to be heard by a disinterested neighbor.

She shivered. "You need to cut your grass. I'm surprised the city hasn't made trouble for you about it."

"No one's complained," he said over his shoulder. "Why does it bother you if I don't cut my grass?"

"You'll get animals, rats and mice. Even—even snakes."

The memory of the Massasauga rattler seized her. She'd run across the snake in the long weeds by the beach. How it had hissed: a sizzling venomous whisper that struck her to the heart. She'd seized a rock and hit it again and again. In its dying throes, it had lashed out and bitten her. Barry had tried to stop her from killing it. Screamed that snakes reduced the insect population and controlled the spread of West Nile virus. Making it clear that the life of a venomous reptile was worth far more than hers.

"Are you all right?" The man had moved over to the refrigerator next to the sink. The freezer door stood open.

She nodded. He was fiddling with a frozen package.

She felt her eyes drawn to it. Through its thick, translucent plastic cover, she could make out dozens of pink, meaty shapes like miniature chicken thighs. "What is that?"

"Pet food," he said. "It's called pinky." He held it out so she could see.

"Oh, my God." The lumps had little legs, heads and tails. "That looks like—that looks like animals."

"Yes, baby mice."

"I'm going to be sick. Washroom. I need the washroom!"

He swore, strode back to the hallway and flung open a door that looked like a panel in the wallboard. She grabbed her purse and charged past him through the opening. And slammed the door behind her.

Acrid bile ate at her throat. She staggered to the toilet. But even in the anemic light from the bare bulb overhead, it looked crusty and foul.

She leaned over the tiny cracked sink, gagging, struggling to breathe.

I will not be sick. I will not be sick.

What the hell did he do with frozen baby mice? Feed them to his cat?

But she hadn't seen a cat.

She twisted the tap over the sink. The water ran rusty at first, then cleared. She splashed some on her face, sipped a little. It tasted faintly metallic.

I need to leave. I've stayed here far too long.

She stared at her reflection in the black-mottled mirror of the medicine cabinet. Now she understood the reason for the wallboard and tight passageway between the kitchen and the large room where he worked and ate. He'd built this washroom between them. So he could live on the first floor forever.

This was where he took a shower, if he washed at all. No windows. No ventilation. Disgusting. And where did he find that horrid pink tub? From the city dump. Where else would he find something so cheap and obsolete?

He'd probably sourced the city dump for everything in this vile house. He wasn't a man, he was a rat. A garbage rat who'd obliterated every vestige of beauty, gnawing and chewing away at it like a malignant parasite to feed his pathological compulsions.

Nothing could save this house. It was a knockdown, a write-off. She'd swing the wrecker's ball herself if she could.

She straightened her coat, hitched up her purse and fumbled for the door handle. Her hands glided over smooth wallboard.

Oh, my God, there's no handle. I'm trapped! He trapped me!

She jostled the door, shoved it. Crashed her weight against it. No luck. Locked. Locked from the outside.

She fumbled through her bag. Found her keys, but her wallet and cell phone were still gone.

He took them, he tricked me.

Her heart went into overdrive. She banged on the door. Shouted for help.

No one can hear me. The house has double brick walls. There's no one outside in the street.

She pounded on the door oblivious to the throbbing pain in her fists. "Let me out! My boss is right outside. My boss—"

She braced her back against door. *I've got to get a grip. Think!* A long black stain was streaking down the centre of the tub.

For a heartbeat, the stain seemed to move. How could that happen? She blinked.

The stain *was* moving. Bleeding down the length of muddy enamel. Heading for the dark hole of the drain.

She gulped air, too terrified to scream. The black fluid swerved away from the drain, rustled up the side of the tub.

Snake! She shrieked in pure terror.

The door opened in a whoosh of air. She crashed out into the blinding light of the kitchen.

"I shouted for help!" She slumped against the fetid counter, breathless as fish out of water. She dared not look behind her for fear of spotting the dark thing slithering out of the tub. "Why—why the hell didn't you open the door?"

"I just did."

"You ignored me deliberately."

"I couldn't hear you. I was in the other room." He held a sheaf of papers in his hand. "The door opens in. You were pushing instead of pulling."

"There's no handle." *And he knew it.*

"Sure there is. Let me show you."

"Stay where you are!" She groped for the dangling scarves of her coat. "I'm leaving. But first I want my wallet and cell phone back!"

He swore. "Give me a minute." He pushed by her and ran down the stairs at the end of the kitchen.

Now, while he's gone.

She stumbled over to the stabbed homunculus and grabbed a knife.

It's only to protect myself.

The knife glided out as smooth as silk. Quickly she slipped it into the side pocket of her coat.

She waited for him again. Waited and waited.

The man wasn't coming back. And he wasn't going to give her back her wallet and phone. Or he'd have done so already. No, he'd tried to fool her into leaving without them.

She crept down the steel-edged stairs to the landing. A set of steep wooden stairs led farther down, away from the landing into the dark. The dark of the basement. That's where he'd taken her things.

That's where that other person was hiding. She dare not confront the two of them together.

She had to get out. Now.

She rushed over to the back door. A brass bolt lock shone there. No key. She'd have to go out the front.

She turned and ran straight into him. He stood at the top of the basement stairs, her cell phone in his fist.

"Is this yours?" He was tall, so much taller than she, his sinewy muscles repellent.

She managed to find her voice. "Where's my wallet?"

"That's going to take time. Give me your phone number. I'll get it back to you."

"Do you expect me to believe you? I need my wallet. Everything's in there. My ID, my credit card."

There must be more money. There must be more money.

"I'm calling the police!" She lunged for her cell phone.

He sidestepped her. For a breathless moment, she hovered on the top stair.

Her spike heels skittered on the rickety steps. She slipped, lost her balance and crashed down. Each step was a fist pummeling a bolt of pain into her. Her arms, legs and ribs were on fire.

She landed on her hands and knees. Earth crunched under her bleeding fingers. The strange smell of the house engulfed her.

She staggered to her feet. Pain shot up from her left ankle.

Light suffused the basement: a humming, blue-white glow leaked from row upon row of opaque white lozenges, glass tanks stretching the full length of the house. The dusty undersides of the floorboards loomed overhead. And heat pressed down on her. Fetid, suffocating heat.

And at the far end, a dark figure scuttled between a row of glowing boxes, bent over, hooded and definitely human. The other person in the house.

They were running an illegal grow-op. All the clues had been there: the heat, the moisture, the strange odors of earth and mildew. Her scalp crawled with fear.

Rationalizations skittered through her mind like ants. *Weed's harmless, legal any day now. Never blame anyone trying to earn a living. We all need money.*

There must be more money. There must be more money.

But her throat closed up, crushing her breath. He'd followed her down. She could sense him behind her, his stale body odor flowed over her.

"You shouldn't be down here," he said.

I've been a fool. Now that I know, they're going to kill me.

"Get away from me!" She shoved her hand into her coat pocket. Clutched the knife.

Behind the milky white panes of the glass tanks, things stirred. Not plants but animals. Restless, moving, twitching, sliding, roiling...

Snakes! An endless sea of snakes, curling and uncurling, forked tongues flickering, dead obsidian eyes watching, fangs glistening in open mouths.

They were dripping over the sides of the tanks, seething over the earth floor, slithering, sliding toward her.

She couldn't scream because she didn't have the breath.

"Don't move." Elongated fingers with bluish nails, gripped her shoulder.

This isn't happening. This isn't happening!

"HAH!" A demon leapt up in front of her. Bristling black hair, a hideously contorted face.

She wheeled back, arms flailing.

"HAH!" A writhing, spotted snake leapt into her face.

She shrieked in a bursting crescendo of terror. Her vision vanished. The knife flew into her hand. She lashed out. Striking again and again.

Light exploded off the blade. Water, water was everywhere. Salt on her tongue. Cries and screams deadened her ears. Her arm pounded down and down. She was savaging the raw flesh of Barry's turkey. Striking again and again.

Ahead, behind, up, down until she was slicing nothing but air.

An icy needle of pain pierced her whirling terror. Deep and agonizing. Striking her leg above her ankle boot.

A pile of clothes on the floor snagged her foot.

She wrenched her leg free. Her arm throbbed with pain from wrist to shoulder.

Red. All she could see was red. A blackish red that clashed with her scarlet coat.

She stumbled toward the daylight streaming down the stairs. Tripped over a fleshy roll of something blocking the bottom step. Her spike heels dug into it before she crawled upstairs.

Memory skittered, jumped and vanished. Images of ice, stairs and falling. She shook with cold. Through the windshield, snow whirled down the middle of the deserted street.

I'm back in my car. How did I get here?

The steering wheel felt sticky under her black-stained hands. A heavy, wet object weighed down her thighs.

The knife.

The throbbing in her leg was agony. She twisted her foot and looked down.

Her calf had swelled enormously, puffing over the top of her broken boot. And there at the edge, two scarlet pinholes.

This can't be happening. I can't breathe.

A bang on the passenger window. "Bella, can't you hear me? Open the door."

Bella stretched out a finger and disengaged the door locks. Even that felt like an effort.

A burst of cold wind: Amelia's musky scent filled her nostrils: seared latte and a sweet whiff of afternoon sex.

Oil of sales glands. Snake oil.

"How did it go?" Amelia asked from the passenger seat.

"I … I think I killed…" Bella panted. She slumped over the steering wheel, clinging to it as though she were being swept away in a current.

Amelia hadn't noticed the stains, the gore. Not yet. She was too busy checking the rear-view mirror. Bella caught a glimpse of tousled blond hair in the reflection. John, her rival, sitting smugly behind the wheel of Amelia's white Mercedes.

"Never mind." Amelia finger waved to John. "It wasn't fair of me to give you such a challenge. But you were keen, so why not? Come on, cheer up. Look upon this as a didactic experience…"

On and on she went, babbling away like a parrot in an echo chamber. Through the drone of her words, Bella watched the sky darken. *Didactic experience—if she says that one more time I'll…*

Amelia's voice ebbed and flowed: "Teardown for sure…professor and his autistic son…" Bella blinked, surfaced. "Son? What did you say?"

"I've known Eric for years. He's a math professor. Didn't I mention that when we were chatting earlier? I'm sure I did." Amelia didn't bother to hide her impatience. "His son is autistic. Eric gave up his life to look after him. That house is destroying them. I thought that you, being older, might relate to Eric better. Persuade him to dump it." She leaned forward. "Is something wrong?"

Laughter erupted in Bella's throat, a bright bubble. She was shaking with it, her shoulders, her thighs, her breasts. "Sn-snake… oil."

"What are you talking about?"

"You knew… they kept snakes."

"Yes, they're therapy for Eric's son."

Bella's vision was closing in. Her lips felt numb. "I told you… I hated snakes, but you sent me…anyway."

"They keep the snakes locked up in the basement. You shouldn't have had a problem."

"A snake bit me." Bella shook her head to ward off the encroaching darkness. "Oh, God…I…I killed them."

"What, you killed the snakes!"

"God, you… never… listen to anyone…but yourself. I killed them. You stupid…fucking bitch, *I killed them!*"

Bella raised the dripping knife. To tear Amelia to pieces as she deserved. But her fingers slid off its handle like jelly. Blood spattered over Amelia's white fur coat.

Amelia screamed. In the distance, Bella heard a door open and someone shout for John. Snow and wind filled the car.

Oh God, what have I done? I killed them. I killed them!

With her last ebbing breath, she lifted her scarlet Medusa's face and howled.

About M.H. Callway

M.H. Callway is the pen name of Madeleine Harris-Callway. In 2013, she and 14 friends together founded the Mesdames of Mayhem.

Madeleine's debut survivalist thriller, *Windigo Fire*, was a finalist for the 2015 Arthur Ellis Best First Novel Award. Her dark suspense novella, *Glow Grass*, first published in *13 O'Clock*, was runner-up for the 2016 AE Best Novella award. Her collected short fiction in *Glow Grass and Other Tales* (Carrick Publishing 2016) ranges from comedy to noir.

An avid runner, cyclist and down-hill skier, she has completed the Toronto Ride to Conquer Cancer every year since it began in 2008. She is currently completing the second book of the Danny Bluestone series, *Windigo Ice*.

Website: www.mhcallway.com
Facebook: www.facebook.com/madeleine.harriscallway
Twitter:@mcallway

KITTY CLAWS TO THE RESCUE

By Rosemary Aubert

You can't teach an old dog new tricks. You can't teach a cat *any* tricks. But sometimes you don't have to. Sometimes cats figure out everything they need to know and then some on their very own.

I guess you could say that my coming to have Kitty Claws was a trick in itself.

I was minding my own business, sitting in my apartment, relaxing, having a little after-dinner drink and reading a mystery novel by my favorite author. I was enjoying a rare moment of silence. No arguments in the vicinity, no rap music, no opera, no doors slamming, no one in the hall shouting plans for when they'd meet again. No gunshots. Not even anybody singing annoying Christmas carols. For it was at Christmas time that she came.

Quiet like that was such a gift that I relished it for the few miraculous minutes that I had it. I knew it wouldn't last long, and I was right. Before long, I heard the pesky dogs down the hall howling away.

And then I heard a cry that would wrench the heart of Ebenezer Scrooge.

I thought at first that it was the cry of a child. Great gasping screams only a few feet from my doorstep sounded through the door itself and echoed down the narrow outer hall, which, though thickly carpeted, seemed to absorb none of the sound.

So, of course, I went to the door and carefully opened it.

The second I did so, the wailing stopped and I found, staring up at me, the most beautiful pair of blue-green cat eyes I had ever seen. I also saw in those eyes a look I'd never seen in an animal before. Odd as it sounds, I'd have called that look *sweet cunning*.

But I only saw it for an instant, because as soon as the little gray-and-white tabby realized that my apartment door was open, she squirted by me and into my living room.

I dove after her, grabbed her and as much as tossed her out the door. I had no idea who she belonged to and I didn't want to take a chance...

But fast as I tried to close the door, she spurted ahead and through it.

She did this three times.

The fourth time, she got right into the living room and pranced across my throw rugs to the far wall. Her head was held high, and her shoulders were poised in an attitude that I can only describe as regal. Her whole body seemed to be saying, "This is very nice. I think I could live here quite comfortably."

I gave up.

She leapt onto my reading chair, curled into a gray-and-white wreath, mewed softly once and fell into a deep sleep.

I waited until the next day to begin my search for her owner. Not that she was any help. As determined as she had been to get into my apartment, she was now determined to stay there. At first I figured she'd be eager to get back to her own home and her own people, but she would have none of it. She wouldn't go anywhere near the door, let alone out of it.

So I had to search without her help.

I knocked on every apartment door on our floor, even the doors of people to whom I usually gave wide berth. I put notices in the elevators, in the mail room, in the laundry room. I even took her picture and posted it on Facebook and on the phone poles near our place.

Facebook was a big mistake, of course. It took me about four minutes to realize that it was a stupid idea for me to try to use it to find Kitty's legitimate owner. I got a bunch of screwy replies, including ones from a whole lot of people who posted pictures of cats that seemed to fit Kitty's description but actually looked nothing like her.

I thought I was being careful not to give too much information about where I lived, but I wasn't sure I had been a hundred percent successful, nor was I certain that I had deleted my message once I changed my mind about it.

I also had a few people from the neighborhood show up at the door. I couldn't believe how stupid I'd been to advertise the way I had.

But, fortunately, after about three days, nobody seemed interested in claiming Kitty.

Yes, *fortunately*, because I soon realized I wanted her for my own.

She was cute, she was cuddly, and best of all, she was clever.

She had a lot of tricks. Whenever I spoke on the phone, she sat beside me and made little mewing noises that sounded as though she were taking part in the conversation. She also liked to sing. Of course, it wasn't real singing, but if I had music—especially a song with words—on the stereo, she seemed to croon along.

Soon I'd made a really comfy bed for her. It was a big basket that I'd found in a second-hand furniture store in my neighborhood. I added a pillow from my own bed and topped the whole thing off with a nice soft white blanket beneath two fluffy towels that I'd been saving in case guests ever came, which they never did.

Kitty seemed to love lying on this and mewing gently before she took her morning nap, her afternoon nap, her just-before-bed-for-the-night nap. You'd think she liked nothing except to sleep, but that soon proved not to be the case.

She had other activities to occupy her time. Anything round that she could get her paws on—an orange in a basket on the table, a ball of fluff from a blanket or a sweater, even a walnut—became a sort of cat soccer ball to be kicked across the floor or out from any nook in which it got caught.

Her dexterity—if you could use that word for a creature without fingers—was remarkable. She seemed able to lift things, to push and to pull. One of her favorite games was to get hold of some small piece of my clothing, drag it from the bedroom or the laundry basket, and hide it between a couple of the layers of her bed in the living room.

She seemed to favor long, silky things: pantyhose, scarves, fabric belts.

I was getting so used to Kitty, to her tricks, to her warmth, to her affection, to her determination to be near me or else to be sleeping peacefully in the little bed I had made for her that I almost forgot how she had come to me, how she wasn't really mine.

So when the pounding knock blasted my door, I had completely forgotten what it probably meant.

There was violence in that knock but no more than I had heard plenty of times from neighbors who'd had a couple too many and didn't realize that my door wasn't their door, from others who thought my music was too loud, from impatient couriers, from the landlord when he had something to demand and was afraid that a tenant was sleeping or hard of hearing or didn't want to hear whatever he had to say.

I didn't open it automatically. Of course I didn't. I walked to the door. I looked out the peephole. At first, it looked as though no one were there. Then I realized that the knocker was so impatient that he was shifting from foot to foot, in and out of the range of the viewer.

I waited until I could get a good look at whoever it was.

I didn't have to wait long until I saw that it was my neighbor from several apartments down the hall. I'd never had much to do with him, partly because he kept to himself and partly because he seemed an unkempt and unpleasant sort of person. Not one I'd really consider a neighbor, just a fellow occupant of our apartment building.

Nonetheless, he wasn't somebody I would ordinarily ignore.

It took me a minute to unlatch the door. Again, I could sense that impatient shifting from foot to foot. And the second the latch came loose, the door swung open with a violence that nearly knocked me off my feet.

"Give her to me! Give me my damn cat!"

I was shocked, but not as shocked as Kitty Claws. She was still and silent for a moment. Then she ran toward him, first hissing, then stopping dead a few feet in front of him. She opened her mouth, and she started the same awful crying and yelling that she had been doing the day I'd found her.

"Quiet, Kitty," I said, but clearly she didn't hear me. She screamed and screamed.

The neighbor's face grew red and his breathing quickened. "Give me the damn cat, you bitch," he shouted, and lunged toward me. As I stepped back to get away, I was afraid I'd trip over the rug at my feet, or even over Kitty, but she suddenly stopped yelling and ran through the apartment and toward the bedroom.

The infuriated neighbor pushed me hard. I fell backward onto the couch and couldn't get up fast enough to stop him from heading after her. When I got there, Kitty was standing near the closet, and the man looked as though he were about to make a grab for her.

Without thinking, I made a grab for him.

That was when I saw that he was holding a knife.

"Get back, you bitch."

All I could think of was Kitty. I dove for her. She wasn't screaming anymore. She was perfectly silent. The reason she couldn't make a sound was that she had one of my scarves in her mouth. It was a pretty one, one of my favorites. I don't know why I should notice a detail like this at a time when Kitty, or me, or both of us were in danger of being attacked by a madman with a knife pointed alternately at each of us.

Like Kitty, I couldn't scream. My mouth was blocked with fear.

I couldn't watch Kitty; I had to watch my neighbor with the knife. He started to wave it. He started to yell. "You damn bitch. Give me back my damn cat."

As terrified as I was, as unable to answer him, to threaten him, even to refuse his demand, I knew I wouldn't give up my sweet little kitten.

Finally, my vocal cords seemed to clear enough for me to utter a single word. "No."

I managed to push past him and to run back toward the living room, toward the apartment door.

He followed me, grabbed my arm and swung me around so that I was staring at him. I saw in his face how truly mad he was. I stepped back, sure I couldn't get away from him, couldn't escape the confines of the living room, let alone the apartment, the hallway, the building.

He held the knife at the level of my heart. Instinctively, I closed my eyes.

I heard the sound of something heavy falling. Had he tripped on the throw rug? My eyes shot open

And I saw he was lying at my feet face down in a pool of spurting blood. The sort of spurt that could only come from an artery. A big artery.

I stared at my pursuer. I could see that he was dead. That instead of plunging his weapon into me, he had tripped and plunged it into himself.

As for Kitty Claws, she quickly disappeared. I heard her mewing in the bedroom, but I soon lost track of her in my rush to call the police.

***

The investigation was swift and conclusive. In his effort to attack me, the man had inadvertently managed to stab himself. It turned out that he had a long record of weapons offenses. He'd been evicted from our building, but had refused to leave; at the time of his death, there had been some sort of warrant to get him out. The fact that there were no fingerprints but his own on the weapon exonerated me, and no charges were laid. "You may not be so lucky next time," one of the cops told me. "It might be you who trips. Get rid of those throw rugs."

Lucky. To have been saved by a rug.

Of course, it took me a while to figure out what had really happened. That this had been no accident. That it was, in fact, a homicide.

And that you can't have a homicide without a murder weapon.

No one but me ever saw the real murder weapon.

I didn't see it at first, either. Until the day I decided to wash the towels and blanket that made up Kitty's bed.

And when I did see it, I realized I hadn't even missed my scarf, only vaguely recalled Kitty circling her former owner and would-be captor. Like the police, I had come to the conclusion that the attacker had tripped on the rug in the living room. A fortuitous accident.

But now I realized that his death had been no accident.

So I thanked Kitty Claws for saving my life—and her own.

And as she lay purring in my lap, I reminded myself, that I had better be careful. It's hard to know you are living with a killer, even when the killer is so darn cute.

About Rosemary Aubert

After a successful career as an internationally-published romance writer, Rosemary Aubert turned to the world of crime, graduating with a Certificate of Criminology from the University of Toronto and publishing the six-volume award-winning, Ellis Portal mystery series. Rosemary also worked in the real world of crime. She was a security officer at the United States Consulate. She ran the office of a half-way house for men coming out of the federal prison system. She served as a Community Relations director assisting women leaving the prison system. And for ten years, she was a bailiff in the criminal courts.

These experiences introduced Rosemary to a wide variety of people—innocent and guilty, dangerous and safe. These denizens of the real world of crime inspired the characters that inhabit her latest book: *The Midnight Boat to Palermo*.

Born in Niagara Falls, New York, Rosemary has long made her home in Toronto, where she has worked as a university instructor, an editor and a bookstore clerk and of course—a writer.

THERE BE DRAGONS

By Jane Petersen Burfield

For a murder, it was both necessary and satisfying. No one had deserved this fate more. No one could threaten her family and get away with it.

She swam in the darkening water as the sky glowed in the west. Soon the fireflies would dance, and she could forget, just for a while, what she had lost and what she had become.

***

"There be dragons," Katie read aloud from the illustration. As she squinted at the map in the old book, the creatures that illustrated the manuscript swirled. A soft green glow lit the map from within. Startled, Katie let the book slip from her fingers onto the dusty desktop.

"We're not supposed to touch that book," Georgie mumbled. Ever since their mother had died, he'd spoken in soft whispers.

"I know, Georgie." She sat in the chair behind the carved oak desk and turned over another page. "Where do you think the dragons lived? I'm not sure I believe in dragons. Maybe they lived a long time ago."

"Of course, there are dragons," Georgie murmured. "Mother told us about them. She showed me one once. I remember going out to the garden with her. We ran around the pond. There was a splashing sound, and a dark shadow came out of the water. A man came out of the trees. Mother pushed me behind her. There was a flash of light, like lightning. I think the man ran away."

"Did you dream that?" Katie closed the book, sending a gentle swirl of dust from the neglected desk flying around the library.

"No," Georgie said hesitantly. "No! I remember. I remember the eyes in the pond. Something chased the man, and then disappeared. I think it was a dragon."

"Well, we could use a dragon now. Creepy Gerry is here bothering Emma. He keeps turning up wherever she is. He follows her. And Dad isn't even aware of it."

"Emma is old enough to look after herself." Georgie peered into the forbidden cupboard in the desk where the book had been.

"No, she's not," Katie said. "She's only 17. And he keeps going after her."

"We'll watch out for her, Katie, and Grandmother Lowe will be here soon. She's scary enough to take care of anything. We'd better get downstairs before Dad finds us up here. He'll be mad if he knows we opened the secret cupboard."

"Okay, Georgie." She put the forbidden book back and locked the cupboard door, closing the outer panel in the desk so it couldn't be seen. "I'll put the key back in Father's drawer later when's he's having coffee in the garden."

"I'll go out with him, Katie. I can keep him away and I love the fireflies."

"You love that garden. Lilacs, lilies, crickets and the fireflies in the trees. Mother loved it too, I remember."

"I really like fireflies the most. They are magical." Georgie headed for the door, listening carefully for anyone outside. In the darkened hall, they turned toward their bedrooms.

***

Peter Drake walked around the dining room to look out on the stone patio. Almost time to summon the kids for supper. Their large stone house sat well back from Barrie Road at the end of a wooded drive. It was very similar to the family home they had left in Wales, complete with dragon gargoyles under the eaves. Now, in the late afternoon, sunlight made the dining room and patio outside a drowsy haven.

He stared at the pond, sitting like a jewel amongst the trees. In certain lights, he swore he could see Maria, but dusk was the best time. The woods were silhouetted against the darkening sky, and the fairy lights danced. He had always loved the little glow bugs that drew him outside. Maria swore they were magical, but he had scoffed at her. Still, unexplained things went on in the garden. Mysteries.

Ginny, their housekeeper, banged the gong for dinner. She loved banging that gong. Ginny had driven Maria mad with the noise, but she had kept their house and lives tidy. How could he deny such a small source of joy to his inherited help?

At dinner, Emma was missing.

"Where's Emma?" Peter asked. "I thought she was home from her weekend with her friends."

"She's tired, Peter. Asked to stay upstairs. I'll take her a tray later," Ginny said as she served plates of salad.

Katie stabbed at a crouton, and it skittered across the tablecloth. "She thinks Cousin Gerry is still here. He left this afternoon, thank heavens. I hope he doesn't come back."

"Gerald asked to visit," Peter said. "We don't have many relatives. I want you to know both sides of your family."

"We know enough about your family, Dad. We don't need to see Gerry." Georgie buttered one of Ginny's soft dinner rolls, ignoring his salad.

"You don't know everything about our family. But I'll tell you more someday when I think you are ready. Now, what did you learn today?"

Living in the country meant that Katie and Georgie had to bus to school and could rarely invite friends over. They had to watch the news or look up a new subject on the computer every day to answer their father's hated ritual question over dinner. He asked every night, trying to be a good parent.

"We learned about China, Dad." Georgie passed the butter to Katie, who was pointing at it as inconspicuously as she could so her father wouldn't get annoyed. "And we looked up some Chinese myths. On Friday, Miss Andrews showed us pictures of dragons in a really neat book. She said they represent power. They were amazing!"

"Dragons are common in many myths and fairy tales. Katie, don't manhandle the rolls." Peter turned back to Georgie. "There are beautiful illustrations in the Lang fairy-tale series. I particularly like the ones in *The Green Fairy Book*. I'll have to find you my copy in the library."

"Sometimes, Dad, I wish they still existed. I almost believe they do."

"Georgie, we talked about that. Evening shadows can make us believe almost anything. But you know they are just shadows."

"But, Dad, I saw one last year. I know I did!"

"Georgie, you have a vivid imagination, just like your mother."

Katie and Georgie looked at their dad in surprise. Peter rarely talked about their mother, and it had been more than two years since her death.

After wiping his chin with his napkin, Peter turned to Katie. "Now what did you learn today?"

She winced and began to recite the trivia she had looked up.

***

After dinner, while Ginny cleaned up, Katie headed outside along the path off the patio. The water in the pond seemed flat black, reflecting the fairy dance of firefly light. She walked farther around the pond as sunset shone through the trees. She wasn't worried about finding her way back to the house after dark. Unusually good night vision was a family trait, her mother had told her. And the house would glow with the lights from the family's rooms.

She looked into the water, hoping to see the shape she had seen so many times before. Tonight, there was nothing there, or nothing she could see. Katie sat down on the bench installed in memory of her mother. She stroked the carved figures on the wooden side, and thought about her. A ripple on the surface of the darkening water drew her eyes away from the silhouette of the house. As the dark waters started to stir, her hopes grew.

"There you are Katie. I thought I'd join you on your walk." The water's surface grew flat again as her father appeared.

Katie took her father's hand and asked, "What really happened that night? The night Mother died?"

Her dad's hand clenched slightly. "Why do you want to know, sweetheart? I've told you what I can."

"You never talk about her or about what happened. All I remember is hearing something across the water. And you ran out. Georgie ran behind you, and I tried to stop him. It was getting very dark. I saw you struggling with someone. He broke away. And then something reared up out of the water, hit the man and swept him in. Something very large. Where was Mother? What happened to her?"

Her dad squeezed her hand. "I know it's confusing. Let's go back to the house." They turned away from the water, and started to walk up the patio to the house. "I think it's time, Katie, for me to tell you what I know. I'm not sure Georgie is old enough yet. Emma knows some of it. We'll find a time to talk tomorrow when we won't be interrupted."

As Katie glanced back at the water, a flicker of light beneath the surface lit a large body in its depths. More flickers of light matched the fireflies above.

***

School the next day seemed interminable. Katie longed to be home for the planned meeting. Emma was waiting for her in the kitchen with juice and Ginny's ginger cookies when she arrived home. Being away at boarding school had changed Emma. She now wanted to spend time with her little sister.

"Do you think he'll tell us about Mother, Em?" Katie asked.

"I hope so, Katie. Don't bug him for details. This is hard for him. You don't see him every night after you and Georgie go to bed. He sits looking out the window at the pond. He can sit there for hours."

"Did he ever tell you what happened? I was young then, just 10, and Georgie was very little. He never said anything to us."

Emma refilled Katie's juice glass. "He rarely talks about Mother. Or the creature."

"So you believe in the creature, too?"

"I do, Katie. I do. It protects us. But the creature knows people are scared of it, so it doesn't often let itself be seen."

"What happened that night? What did you see?"

"I'm not sure, Katie. I saw something, but I'm not sure what. A man grabbed Mother outside on the patio. He dragged her around the pond. Then something hit him as he held her. I swear it looked like an animal claw. Then it got really confusing."

The girls heard the front door open and their father call for Ginny. They listened to him settle in the dining room, where they knew he would be looking out the window, even though dusk wouldn't fall for another few hours. They looked at each other, and went quietly to join him.

"Hello, my little ones. How was your day?" He poured himself a whiskey.

"The usual, Dad," said Emma.

"Same here" said Katie. "Are we going to talk about Mom before Georgie gets home from soccer?"

"Yes, I guess so. We should." He walked over to close the dining room door, and sat at the table, his back to the windows. "I'm not sure where to start. There are things about your mother's side of the family that few people know. But someone found out, and Maria had to be protected."

"Who threatened her? You've never told us this," Emma said.

"Your mother was…special. Her family goes back a long way in Wales. They were never rulers, but ruler makers. And they had some unusual abilities."

"Like what, Dad?" Katie asked.

"They were—they are—deeply connected to the old world, to the magical side that most people have forgotten about or scoff at. They understand magic. And because of that, they are in danger."

"So that's why we left Wales." Emma held Katie's hand tightly in her own.

Peter got up from his chair and came around the shining wood table to stand near them. Taking both their hands, he said, "Yes. Your mother had to leave for her safety. We brought your grandmother and your great-grandmother with us. We thought we'd all be safer over here, but they found us. They sent a man to try to kidnap your mother."

"Who are *they*?" Emma asked.

"I'm not sure. I believe they belong to another old family who knows the secrets of power. The man that night tried to capture your mother. She decided she needed to keep you safe."

"How?" Katie turned to look at the pond.

"Your mother knew you would be in danger if they knew she was still alive." Peter looked at the girls. "What I'm going to tell you now is a secret, a very important secret. Your mother vanished to protect you. The police believe that she fell or was pushed into the pond, but they never found her body. They only found blood on a rock nearby and ripped material from the dress she was wearing on the rocks and bushes where the water cascades down to the lake. They think her body was swept out of the pond into the lake. The water runs pretty fast over the cliff, especially when it rains."

"What about the man? Did he drown in the pond, too?"

Peter shifted in his chair, to half face the water. "They never found him. The police thought he may have survived. That he climbed out of the pond at the far end."

"But so could Mother!" Emma got up to stand by the fireplace where she could see his half-turned face.

"We thought it best for your sake to say she died. I don't know if we were right."

"Is Mother still alive?" Katie sat with her shoulders coat hanger-straight, clutching the arms of her chair, looking at her father with wide-open eyes.

"No one is to know what I've told you. Including Georgie. He's too young. You all will be in great danger if this becomes known."

They heard the front door open, and Ginny's cheerful voice bounce down from the front hall. "Hello. Anyone here? Oh, there you are." She peeked into the dining room. "I'll put the kettle on and make a quick dinner."

When she'd gone, Peter said: "We'll talk more about this another time, girls. It's important that you know. Remember, keep the information secret."

∗∗∗

Katie was glad to go upstairs with Emma. Their mother was, seemingly, alive. And if she hadn't died, where was she? When could they see her?

"Katie, I want to show you something." Emma pulled her sister into her bedroom. "After mother disappeared, I found her jewelry box hidden at the back of her closet. And in it, I found this." She held up a very old necklace—a dark red stone shining from an intricately woven gold shield, hanging on a long rose-gold chain. "I think this is what the intruder wanted. I don't know what to do with it now. I'm nervous to leave it in the house."

"Wow, Em." The necklace shone with more brilliance than the window light should have given it. Katie examined it, holding the chain so the pendant flashed. "But why did you take it?"

"I wanted something that was Mother's. Sometimes I wear it under my top."

157

"Be careful, Em. Put it back in the closet. Dad might look for it now that he's told us about Mother."

"No, he won't. He doesn't like to look at anything that reminds him of her. He doesn't even go into the living room, because her picture above the fireplace makes him sad."

Katie shook her head and walked over to Emma's window. "I don't know what to think about what Dad told us. If Mother is alive, where is she?"

She looked out at the pond, but nothing was stirring.

***

Peter, too, looked out toward the pond in late afternoon sun. Had he been wise to tell the girls? But if anything happened to him, they needed to know.

He knew she was in the water, benign and protective, but he had never seen her. The ability to see the magic was given only to Maria's daughters. Neither he nor Georgie could see her. He could hear her, and occasionally he saw a shadow move. Nothing more.

***

Dinner was very silent, except for Georgie talking about the upcoming school play. Peter for once did not question them about what they'd learned that day.

After dinner, Katie waited in the dark hallway outside the dining room. When Peter stepped onto the patio, and walked toward the sunset-lit trees around the pond, she followed him.

Fireflies, lively tonight, hovered between tree branches and above the pond. And in the water, light seemed to shine upward.

"Ah, Katie. It's a beautiful evening. I thought some fresh air might clear my head."

"May I walk with you, Dad? I've finished my homework."

"Of course. How are you feeling about what I told you today?"

"Why is all this happening to our family? Why are the people coming here, coming after us? And where is Mother now?"

"They think your mother—and now perhaps you and Emma—know about something they want. It's hard to explain. The women in our family are special. They have special sight, and special abilities." He took Katie's hand. "Have you ever seen anything...peculiar...in the pond? A creature?"

Katie looked up at her dad. "I know there is something in the pond. I've never seen it clearly, but I know it's there."

"You do have the special sight, then, Katie."

"Georgie says it saved us from the strange man before Mother disappeared."

"I was surprised when Georgie said he saw something. Usually only the women have the sight. Maybe young children do, too."

"Where did this creature come from, Dad? I'm not afraid of it."

"The creature is a female, like you and Emma, and your mother. It's part of your heritage, your Welsh family."

"Can Emma see her?"

"Yes, she has the sight, too. You both see many things other people don't. Have you ever tried to talk to the creature?"

"Sort of, Dad. Once I sang a lullaby Grandma Lowe used to sing to us. One that Mother knew. There was a ripple. It was too dark to see, but I wasn't afraid."

"You were singing to your great-grandmother. We brought her with us from Wales, but she got very sick on the journey, and so she left her human form. She's the creature, the dragon in the pond. She is powerful and protects you, indeed all of us. There is still danger for her, though. Few people believe that dragons still exist, but..."

"Why do those other people want to hurt us?" Katie slipped her hand back into her father's as they reached the far side of the pond. From there, the sun reflected on and through the water, and she saw the large, dark shape, followed by a smaller shape.

Peter stopped and looked intently at her. "There is a book, a valuable book that belongs to our family. We brought it with us from Wales, and I hid it in the house. It's about dragons. In the historian world, it would cause a sensation."

"I know about the book, Dad. It's beautiful. The pages shine."

Peter glanced quizzically at her, but continued. "There's also a pendant made from a rough garnet set in Welsh gold. It goes with the book. Strange things happen when the two are close to each other, so I hid them in two different places. I think that's what the men are after. I don't know how they found out about them, because only our family knows."

Katie and Peter sat down on the memorial bench, Peter's fingers automatically searching to rub the inscription to Maria.

"Did you tell Cousin Gerry about it, Dad?"

"Yes, unfortunately. Yes, I did."

"Dad, I don't know how to say this. I've seen him in the upper hallway, several times, where he has no right to be. He spies on us. And he follows Emma. I don't like him at all. Neither do Emma and Georgie."

Peter sighed and looked into the water. "Gerry's never been as reliable as he could be. But I thought, I hoped, he would protect our family if need be. It's possible he's behind it. I hope not. But I don't know."

"Is there anyone else who knows?"

"Just your Grandma Lowe. I've left a letter for our lawyer in case something happens to me. Other than that, we've told no one. I think Ginny suspects something, but I don't want to put her in danger. She's a good woman. I'll be glad when Grandma Lowe returns from Wales."

The water rippled, and a black tail tip emerged.

"It's time." Peter stood up and brought out a silver whistle. "Would you like to meet your great-grandmother, Katie? I mean, meet her again. You knew her in Wales when you were very little."

"I remember her. Oh, yes, Dad. I would."

Peter blew one long note on the whistle. Suddenly, a dark green head emerged from the water, followed by a scaled back, bright wings and a pointed tail.

"Margaret, here is your great-granddaughter, Katie."

The creature pulled herself up onto a rock, and spoke in a gravelly voice. "Hello, little one. You have grown since I last talked with you."

"Great-grandmother! I am so glad to see you. I wish Mother were here, too."

The dragon moved closer to Katie and her father. An ethereal wing wrapped around the girl's shoulders, nudging Peter aside. He looked startled, but then moved back.

"Well, little one, your mother is not too far away. I tell her how you are and what you are doing. She so much wants to come back to you. But your father and I decided that for everyone's safety, she should stay hidden. Like the locket and the book. I know you have seen both. Keep them separate, and keep them safe."

"Margaret, I wish I could see you." Peter looked in the direction of the rock beside the bench. "I'm grateful for your protection of the children."

"I will always protect my little ones, Peter. Don't worry."

Katie watched as she unwrapped her wing. She slid off the rock, and back into the water. Just before her head went under, she said, "Remember, keep the treasures safe. I'll be here."

***

The rest of the week slipped by quickly. Emma and Katie would quietly ask their dad questions, but he rarely answered them, pretending Ginny or Georgie were about to enter the room.

On Thursday night, Ginny called Peter to the phone.

"Hi, Peter. It's Gerry. I'd like to come down."

"Gerry. We're busy this weekend. Perhaps another time?"

"I need to see you. Now."

"Sorry. As I said, we are busy. The kids are in a play at school. Before their holidays begin." Peter listened as the receiver slammed down. He hoped not to hear from Gerry again.

***

Katie was glad the school year was almost over. On Friday afternoon, she went upstairs to put on her costume and asked Emma for help with her makeup.

Emma applied mascara to Katie's lashes, and stood back to study her handiwork. "Beautiful. You are growing up fast."

"I wish Mother could see me." Katie looked into the old dresser mirror, through silvered reflections, imagining what she would look like in a few years. Her mother's dress, hemmed up with tape and held in by a belt, outlined her maturing shape. Her copper hair had darkened over the winter, but the summer sun would lighten it back to a blaze. Her green eyes were her mother's color. She glowed, much like the afternoon sun outside the window.

Trailing skirts just a bit too long for her, Katie stepped down the stairs, surprised to see her father at the bottom. "You look so much like your mother, Katie. I'm not surprised you have her gift."

"Thanks, Dad." She paused on the stairs, aware of a new feeling. Power? Could it be power? "We should go. Is Ginny in the car?"

"Yes, ready to go." Peter called up the stairs. "Georgie!"

"Coming, Dad." The small boy tumbled past Katie on the stairs. His old-fashioned suit, expertly recut by Ginny from Peter's old jacket, made him look like he had stepped out of a movie. "I'm excited."

"I know, son." Peter locked the front door, and they left for the school.

Nearby, watching them go, was a man dressed in black.

***

The play—a re-enactment of village life 150 years ago during Canada's Confederation—was a success. As the audience clapped for their own children, if not for other cast members, Katie fought an urge to get home. She didn't want to stay for the reception and the congratulations, the groups of neighbors gossiping, the kids running to burn off energy after sitting still for an hour. She just wanted to go home.

After a few minutes of lemonade, cookies and chat, she whispered to Peter that something was wrong. He looked at her, this little die-cut version of Maria, and knew they must go. Ginny rounded up Georgie while Emma, Katie and Peter headed outside to their car.

The drive through the darkening woods was silent. Even Georgie seemed to feel anxious now. As they turned down their long driveway, a light shone from the far side of the house.

Peter told everyone to stay in the car. He got out and ran around to the back. When he didn't return, Emma scrambled out the door, followed by Katie. Ginny kept Georgie with her inside the car.

The girls ran around the house to the patio. The dining room door stood open, the glass in shards on the ground. Inside, Peter was wrestling with a man.

Katie tried to run in to help. Emma held her back, but Katie broke free. She shot inside and leaped on the man's back. He tried to shift her, but she hung on. Peter hit him hard. Katie and the man fell to the carpet.

Peter pulled Katie up and hugged her. She could feel him shaking. He collapsed in a chair, while Georgie and Ginny burst into the dining room. Emma dialed 911 for the police.

"What happened? Who is he?" Georgie pushed away from Ginny and tried to pull off the man's mask off before Peter grabbed him.

On the floor, the intruder groaned, then stirred.

"Find some rope, or duct tape," Peter ordered. "Emma, did you call the police? Katie, go to the front to wait for them. Georgie, stay back."

Suddenly, the intruder scrambled up and dug into his pants pocket. A glittering knife appeared in his right hand. He lunged for Georgie and grabbed him. Keeping an eye on Peter, he dragged Georgie by the boy's collar across the room to the outer door. "Don't come any closer, Peter.

Give me the book and the necklace and I'll leave. I'll keep Georgie with me. Give them to me or he'll die."

"Gerry!" Peter recognized the intruder's voice. "Why are you doing this? These are my children!"

"Money, Peter. Just money." He yanked Georgie to his feet with his left hand. "You have valuable things. With Maria dead, you don't need them anymore. And I do."

"I can't believe you'd betray us like this, threaten my kids."

"You heard me." Gerry moved back, a firm hold on Georgie. "Give me the book and the necklace or Georgie will get hurt." He brandished the knife. "I mean it."

Suddenly, Georgie kicked backward hard, striking Gerry in the shin. Gerry yelled in pain and loosened his grip on the boy's collar. Georgie broke free and rushed out the dining room door.

Katie watched Georgie run toward the bench on the far side of the pond with a cursing Gerry, knife still in hand, in close pursuit. She rushed after them. Georgie and Gerry were beside the water, with Gerry closing the gap between him and the boy. Then, to her amazement, she saw a large golden claw come out of the water. Gerry turned, his eyes widened, and he dropped the knife. The claw reached up, hooked Gerry and dragged him under.

Katie screamed. Light shot up into the sky like fireworks. The water surface quivered with the struggle beneath.

Peter and Emma came running up to her. Katie could only point. Georgie shouted about Gerry in the now-quiet pond.

"Georgie, listen to me," Peter said, spotting the knife and pocketing it. "The police will be here soon. Tell them Gerry fell into the water."

"Yes, sir," said Georgie.

He turned to Katie. "You understand, don't you, Katie? Do not tell them what you saw. Say the same thing."

Katie nodded. Looking at the water surface, now lit by fireflies, she couldn't believe anything had happened. The surface, as smooth and dark as oil, reflected the last of the sunlight. At the far end of the pond, she saw two dark shapes emerge from the water and, with a swirl of wings, lift into the sky.

She heard running footsteps, and knew the police were close. And as they arrived at the pond, she saw two magnificent dragons, one large, and one smaller, fly through the twilight, and out over the trees. She shivered as fireflies danced around her. She knew she had just seen her mother and knew she would see her again. Then she could see nothing but the last of the twilight, shining through the trees.

***

Later that night, after having Ginny's restorative cups of cocoa, the girls relaxed in Emma's bedroom. Emma hugged Katie and pulled the garnet pendant out from under her blouse. Soft light infused the space around them.

"That was quite a day, Katie."

"I'm so glad it's over. I'm glad Mother is alive. I'm glad there's some magic in the world. Most of all, I'm glad we're safe again." Katie settled back down on the bed.

The sisters smiled as the pendant lit up, fire-like. They would keep it and the book safe. They would keep their family safe.

And soon, Katie knew, they would see what happened when they put the pendant and the dragon book together.

About Jane Petersen Burfield

To her utter amazement, Jane won the Bony Pete Short Story Award in 2001 for "Slow Death and Taxes", the first short story she wrote. After several more years of success with the Bloody Words story contest, she has had several more short stories published in the anthologies, *Blood on the Holly*, *Thirteen* and *13 O'Clock*. Her story in the Edgar Allen Poe tribute anthology, *Nevermore*, won critical praise.

Killing someone softly with words is greatly appealing to a North Toronto matron like Jane. She regards finding a way to use fashion, vegetables and small animals in her stories to bring about justice, albeit rough justice, a challenge and an adventure.

Connect with Jane Burfield at her Website
www.janeburfield.com
Or on Facebook

THAT DAMN CAT

By Marilyn Kay

Detective Constable Maureen Kelly carefully placed the phone receiver in its cradle. She took a deep breath and exhaled slowly to stop her throat from tightening.

"Looks like the AMBER Alert is off," she announced. "They think they've found the body."

Silence enveloped the Homicide squad room. The team had been investigating fatal shootings and stabbings since May, and now they had to deal with the murder of a *child*.

Detective Constable Joe Corso breezed by with his usual tight-butt swagger, apparently not noticing that he'd dropped the car keys into her macchiato. He looked over his shoulder. "Come on, Mo, let's go. We're heading down to Williamson Park Ravine. Lou wants us there, pronto."

Maureen rolled her eyes and mopped up the spill. Why did their boss, Detective Sergeant Lou Harvey, always brief Joe first? Her glare shut down the titters of her colleagues.

She pulled on her jacket, picked up her clutch and pocketed her phone. "Yeah all right, Curly Joe," she muttered as she headed to the car. She knew getting stuck with this clown was the trial by fire for every new recruit in the Homicide unit. Once this was over, she hoped to get paired with someone smart, like Detective Constable Jennifer Blake.

The weather had stayed warm this September, and a misty rain had left the trees glistening, their leaves tinged with gold and red.

Williamson Park Ravine was part of the Small's Creek ravine system in Toronto's east end. The city's parks department had recently manicured the Gerrard Street East entrance and added a wooden staircase leading down into the ravine. There, underneath the steps, was a black industrial-size garbage bag containing the naked body of 13-year-old Caitlyn Jones, missing since last Friday.

The investigative team was securing the scene, and had begun marking out and photographing footprints and possible drag marks. Footprints on the stairs had already been lifted to enable the team easier access to the ravine.

Maureen pulled back her unruly, shoulder-length auburn hair, and slipped on crime-scene gloves and slippers before joining Lou and Forensic Identification Officer Mark Madden at the bottom of the stairs.

She knew what Lou was going to say even before he handed her the address. She and Curly Joe had the job of informing the bereaved family. She bit her lip and squared her shoulders. This was her first time informing a family of a death, and she was stuck with an insensitive jerk to see it through.

***

Maureen and Joe didn't leave Caitlyn's distraught parents until she had arranged for Mrs. Jones's sister to stay with them.

"Hey, Mo! You did good," Joe said on their way to the station. "Mrs. Jones was a mess, but you pulled it off okay. How 'bout I treat you to a macchiato before we head back to the squad room?"

Maureen wrinkled her nose. "No thanks, Joe. Another time." *You useless moron.* But as soon as she'd parked the car, she took off to pick up a Starbucks before returning to her desk.

She arrived just in time to hear Lou—standing with his sleeves rolled up and his right thumb jutting out of his pants pocket—brief the team.

"Initial forensic findings indicate Caitlyn was electrocuted," Lou said. "There were signs of low-voltage burns on other parts of her body. She also suffered at least one sexual assault."

Bile burned Maureen's throat and mouth; she wished she hadn't bought that Starbucks coffee.

Lou continued, "Her probable time of death was sometime on the Sunday night. Recovered nail scrapings and some fine cement dust powdering parts of her body indicate possible confinement in an unfinished or partially finished basement or a garage.

"We're extending door-to-door canvassing to the neighborhoods surrounding the entire Small's Creek ravine network."

As an afterthought, he added, "A further consideration is to look for cats. Forensics found cat dander and a few long orange cat hairs stuck in Caitlyn's dark brown hair."

"So we'll be interviewing all the cats in the neighborhood, too?" Joe quipped. There was a collective groan. But as Lou allocated assignments, Maureen could see crooked smiles on a number of her colleagues' faces as they grabbed their notebooks and proceeded to their tasks.

Lou wanted Maureen and Joe to reinterview the families of Caitlyn's friends, as well as talk to staff and members of the Fairmount Park Community Centre, where she used to hang out.

"Joe, let's do a quick run-through of those initial interviews before going back to see the families, shall we?" Maureen said.

"Sure, if you want. But maybe we should head over to the Fairmount Centre first. We didn't talk to them last time."

"Fair enough. Give me five and I'll be ready."

The urge to get to the Ladies suddenly overwhelmed Maureen. She felt clammy all over, and her armpits dripped with sweat. Her tautly muscled, five-foot-seven-inch body went wobbly; she clutched the toilet seat and vomited.

This wasn't the way a police detective was supposed to act.

Still trembling a bit, she rinsed out her mouth, splashed water on her face and wiped mascara drips from around her hazel eyes. She fixed her hair into a low ponytail, adjusted her clothes and popped the last mint from her purse into her mouth before emerging from the washroom.

"You want me to drive, Mo?"

She was about to snap at him, but instead handed him the keys. "Yeah. Okay."

"Your first child murder. It's always the hardest. So let's get that fucker! Right?"

Maureen nodded. "That's why I joined Homicide."

***

They finished late, but still had no leads as they parted ways and headed home. Maureen walked over to her favorite Thai takeout on Yonge Street, while Joe went home to microwave his supper.

Joe was the only guy—make that the only detective—she knew who cooked up spaghetti and meatballs—or whatever else he ate—and packaged the food into frozen meals ready to microwave whenever he got home.

As Maureen looked at her gelatinous *pad thai*, she wondered if his home-cooked meals were the secret to his still-trim, well-muscled figure. Many of her colleagues were overweight after years of takeout and irregular eating. She wasn't going to let that happen to her. At 27, she was as strong and as fit as when she had passed the Physical Readiness Evaluation for Police test with flying colors five years ago. The thought of going to her condo gym briefly crossed her mind, but sheer weariness canceled that idea. She dumped the rest of her takeout in the compost bin and went to bed.

***

Over the next two days, Maureen and Joe knocked on doors to interview people who hadn't been at home when they'd previously called and talked to more volunteer staff at the community center—all with no success. No one had seen Caitlyn or anything suspicious.

***

Connie Abbott opened the sliding glass door and gazed at the stars twinkling between the passing clouds. She stuck her hand out the door and shook a bag of cat treats.

"Maxie! Maxie! Come to Mama!" she cajoled.

Her husband Sam's heavy six-foot-two-inch frame loomed behind her. He gripped her shoulder.

"Will you shut that door? That damn cat will be fine out there. Hell, he's big enough to fend for himself."

Connie winced, then lightly placed her hand on his. "Oh Sam, don't be so impatient. Maxie's just doing what every tom does, hunting and prowling for a lady love."

She shut the door and gave Sam's grizzled cheek a peck. "There. No need to be jealous. I'll give Maxie 15 more minutes. He'll be ready to come in by then."

Sam gave her butt a sharp whack that made Connie flinch. "I'm going to bed, then. Don't be long."

"I'll just finish my cup of tea and get the cat in. Keep the bed warm for me."

She set the bag of treats on the kitchen table, settled her ample thighs onto a chair and sat cradling the mug of chamomile tea. At 55, her figure had expanded to the point where she looked like everybody's favorite aunt.

She and Sam could never have children, so they had settled for cats. Maxie was their third, and Connie's favorite.

Shrieks and yowls pierced the night air.

She peered through the glass of the door to see a mass of shaggy hair galloping toward the kitchen. Maxie was through the door in a flash, overturned his kibble bowl and hid under the living room sofa. Treat bag in hand, Connie followed him. With a groan, she crouched down and proffered him a treat.

"Got yourself in a tangle, big boy?"

Maxie's fat, tufted paw knocked the treat onto the floor before he gobbled it up.

She held out another treat.

Maxie, his amber-green eyes wide in his furry face, stared before he began to wash his face.

"Okay. Looks like you're fine." Connie dropped the treat on the rug, got up and went back to the kitchen to refill his bowl. Then, with a glance in Maxie's direction, she headed off for bed.

***

On Thursday, Lou assigned Maureen and Joe to do some follow-up canvassing on Woodycroft Road. There were more bungalows there, rather than the semidetached homes more predominant on other streets in the area.

Woodycroft also had a small entrance to the Small's Creek ravine system.

As they crossed over to Woodycroft, Maureen saw what at first looked like an orange raccoon with a bushy tail trundling across the lawns. She nudged Joe. "Cat! The right color." She pointed as the cat turned its squarish face towards them. "Shall we see where it's going?"

Joe put his right hand to his brow and swiveled his head. "Let's go stalk that cat."

Maureen grinned.

They followed the cat for almost the length of the street before it hopped up some stairs and settled onto the porch of the bungalow at 106 Woodycroft. As they approached, their phones pinged simultaneously.

Maureen took photos of the cat and the nearby houses, then looked at her text. Another teenage girl was missing. Twelve-year-old Anastasia Voulos was thought to be somewhere in the vicinity. She opened the brief on her phone while Joe called Lou.

Anastasia's mother, Sophia, a nurse at Toronto East General Hospital, had expected her daughter to meet her at 6 p.m. in the hospital lobby. They had planned to go to the Danforth for dinner to celebrate the divorce settlement between her and Anastasia's father, Konstantine. Sophia feared that her ex-husband had kidnapped Anastasia, as he had threatened to do more than once. Her daughter's phone security app indicated she was in the vicinity of Woodycroft Road, before her phone shut off. Konstantine, who now lived with his mother in a semidetached house on Woodycroft Road, had called in sick that morning.

Maureen and Joe were to proceed immediately to 2 Woodycroft Road and check out Konstantine Voulos.

They could hear the hacking even before they knocked on the door.

A woman—presumably Voulos's mother—opened the door.

"Kosta, the police again. They want to talk to you," she called out and went back to the kitchen.

A sneezing Voulos came to the door. "*More* cops! What do you guys want now?"

Maureen tilted her head away from Voulos's spray. "May we come in, Mr. Voulos? We have a few more questions to ask you."

Voulos motioned them inside. "I told the other guys I knew nothing about the girl or the neighbors. I'm only here till I get a place of my own."

"This time we'd like to ask you about your daughter, Anastasia," Maureen said. "Your *wi*—her mother—thinks she might be here. With your—and your mother's—permission, we'd like to search your home."

"Here? What would she be doing here? Go ahead! Search the place. What game is Sophia playing now?"

"This is not a game, Mr. Voulos," Maureen replied. "Your daughter has gone missing and her phone app pinpointed her whereabouts to somewhere in this vicinity."

Voulos covered his face and erupted into another bout of coughing. "Oh…my…God! Anastasia? No. She must be with a friend."

While Maureen continued the interview, Joe searched the house and grounds. No Anastasia.

Promising to keep Voulos updated, they left him spluttering, while his mother poured coffee and opened a tin of cookies.

The sun was setting, and it was getting a bit chilly.

As they walked back up the street, Maureen mused, "Lou told you Jennifer spoke to a woman who thought she'd seen a girl with long dark hair around 5:30. The girl was waiting at the Coxwell bus stop near Fairford Avenue going north."

"Yeah. She talked to a lady with a cat carrier. Blond, short and plump I think Jennifer said."

"So did they both get on the bus?" Maureen asked.

"The woman didn't know," Joe said. "She left the parkette before the bus arrived."

"Hmm. So could the cat lady be implicated in Anastasia's abduction?"

"Maybe. That's why I told Lou I'd text him with the address if a woman of that description answered the door."

"Here's the house where we saw the cat on the porch."

"Let's see what a few close neighbors have to say first."

***

They had no luck with neighbors immediately to the left and right of the house. But at the house two doors up the street, a harried-looking elfin woman opened the door, glanced at their badges and invited them in. A baby carriage on the porch signaled the woman could be a good source of information, since new mothers usually walked around their areas a lot with their infants and were often up at all hours of the night.

Dora Otley hadn't noticed any strange goings-on in the neighborhood, but she had plenty of grievances about her next-door neighbors and the noise and dust from their home renovations. "They were my best friends on the street, until they started excavating. Then they added a gross gray hulk onto the house that nearly cuts off access to our side door."

She also wasn't happy about the caterwauling of stray cats fighting at night. "I just get to sleep, then the screeching begins and the baby starts to wail again."

Maureen nodded. "I can sympathize, Mrs. Otley." She paused. "Are all the cats around here strays, or do some have owners?"

"Connie has a big Maine Coon. But he's a doll. And Connie is, too. She babysits Emma when I have an appointment or I need a break. In fact, I don't know what I'd do without Connie this week with Randy away with a client in New York."

"When did Randy leave?" Maureen asked.

"He took Porter's 8 a.m. flight on Monday."

"And he returns?"

"Tomorrow night. He'll probably be home by around 8:30."

"Okay. Could you tell me more about Connie, please?"

"Sure. Actually, everyone I know loves Connie Abbott. She's always cheerful and helpful. Her husband Sam upgraded our house's electrical system and gave us an amazing deal."

Maureen gave a nod to Joe. "Ah. And where do Connie and Sam reside?"

"Oh, two doors down at 106. I think Sam's still working, but Connie should be in."

Joe pulled out his phone and began to text.

They got up to leave.

"Thank you, Mrs. Otley," Maureen said. "You said your husband will be home around 8:30 tomorrow? We'd like to have a chat with him, too, when he gets back from New York. Please let him know."

As they walked down the porch steps, Joe said, "Lou's got the address. Now let's see if Connie Abbott is at home."

"Wait a minute, Joe. I want to take a quick look at the reno job. Remember, there was cement dust on Caitlyn's body and under her nails."

The two nosed around the vacant house that Mrs. Otley complained had been swarming with builders earlier in the day. Only a white van remained. Satisfied they'd seen enough, they went over to the Abbotts' home.

Connie came to the door at the second knock.

Maureen and Joe showed their badges.

"Mrs. Abbott, I'm Detective Constable Joe Corso and this is Detective Constable Maureen Kelly, Toronto Police. We're doing some door-to-door canvassing in connection with the death of Caitlyn Jones. She was found dead Monday in the Williamson Park Ravine. May we come in?"

Connie scrutinized their badges for a moment, then motioned them in. "Sure...of course."

Maureen looked at the plump bottle blonde dressed in stretch pants and a red tunic sweater, and saw nothing remarkable

"Come in and make yourselves comfortable," Connie said.

Maureen sat down on a big wingback chair.

"Oh no. That's the cat's chair," Connie chided. "Sit down over there on the sofa. I think it's clear of hair."

Maureen stood up, brushed her backside and sat beside Joe on the sofa.

"Would you care for a cup of tea?" Connie offered. "I drink mostly herbal, but I think I can rustle up some ordinary black tea bags. Or would you care for some instant coffee?"

"No thanks, Mrs. Abbott," they both intoned.

Connie sat down on a big easy chair. "Oh please, call me Connie. Everyone else does."

Joe pulled out his notebook, his signal to Maureen to handle the questioning.

"Mrs. Otley was just telling us about your cat," Maureen began.

"Oh, Maxie? I'm afraid he's populated the ravine with little Maxies and Maxines. Dora's not so happy about that. But boys will be boys, and Maxie is a very big boy."

Maureen glanced around. "Is he around now? I love cats, too."

"*Noo*. I'm not sure where he is right now. But he'll be scratching at the back door when he gets hungry."

"Right. Well, we'd like to ask you and your husband a few questions. By the way, where is Sam now?'

Connie nestled her thighs a bit more in the chair, half shut her eyes and rubbed her upper lip against her lower one. "Oh, he won't be back until 8:30 or nine tonight."

"Why so late?"

"Well, he's got a big job out in Oshawa. And it can be a bitch of a drive—pardon my French—back into the city."

"What does your husband do?"

"Sam's an electrical contractor. He upgraded Dora and Randy's house. I asked him to give them a good deal, and he did."

Then Maureen asked Connie where she had been around five o'clock.

"I found a little Maxine limping around and decided to take her to ORA on Coxwell. You know, the Organization for the Rescue of Animals? They're good with rescuing cats."

"That was very kind of you, Connie. What time do you remember getting there?"

"Well, it's just a short streetcar ride to Coxwell, then a quick walk down to their building. I'm not sure. I was home before six."

"When you walked down Coxwell to ORA or back to the Gerrard streetcar, did you talk to anyone?"

Connie giggled. "Sam says I jabber to everyone."

"Do you remember talking to a teenage girl with long dark hair?"

Connie appeared to consider the question. "I may have. But if I did, I wouldn't remember. I was more concerned about the cat."

Maureen took her phone from her clutch, scrolled for a moment, then handed the phone to Connie. "Could I ask you to look at this photo and see if you remember?"

Connie squinted at the photo for a long time before returning the phone to Maureen. Then she shook her head slowly. "Nope. There wasn't anyone like her on the streetcar."

"I'm talking about *before* you got on the streetcar, Connie. We've got a report from another person who thought she saw someone very much like you talking to this girl. Does that help jog your memory?"

Connie put her hand to her neck, then quickly withdrew it. "What are you talking about? I thought you were here to talk about that poor girl, Caitlyn Jones. Now you're showing me a photo of someone I've never seen before, and telling me I saw her before getting on the streetcar."

"I thought I said someone *very much like you*, Connie. It's important that you think hard about this girl because she's gone missing. We'd like to find her before something bad happens to her."

"Well, I can't tell you what I don't know."

"Perhaps you'd like to think more about it. We can come back when your husband gets home."

"Thanks for your time, Mrs. Abbott," Joe said as he and Maureen got up to leave. "We can see ourselves out."

As they walked toward the street, Joe asked, "Well, what do you think?"

"Call it a hunch, but I think Anastasia is in there," Maureen replied.

"Yeah. I'd say Connie's hiding something."

Joe pulled out his phone. "Let's Google the ORA." He searched for a moment, then said, "They're open until nine tonight. We can swing by and see if they corroborate Connie's story. By the way, Lou is sending some surveillance to help us out."

"Okay, Joe, let's go."

***

Maureen swung the car into the ORA building's parking lot.

"You want to do the talking this time?" she asked.

"Nah! You're on a roll, Maureen. Go for it."

A volunteer, Pete, remembered having seen Connie. "Yeah! She handed in an injured cat about five this evening. I've logged it. It's right here. Do you want to see the cat?"

"No thanks," Maureen said. "Do you mind if I take a photo of your log page?"

"Go ahead."

As Maureen thanked Pete and took a picture, Joe handed him a card. "Write your name and telephone number where you can be reached on the back, please. We'd like to get back to you real soon."

***

"It's nearly eight, Joe," Maureen said as they pulled up across the street from the Abbott home. "I bet her husband is already home. In fact, I think he was at home all the time we were there."

Joe threw up his hands. "Okay, Mo! How the hell do you know he's in there?"

"I thought his van was the one parked at the reno up the street," she said as they stepped out of their car.

"What? I didn't see any logo or lettering on it," Joe said as they headed toward the house.

"But it would make sense he would get the job," Maureen countered. "Dora Otley would have recommended Abbott to her now *ex*-best friends. Besides, I checked on the license plate number. The van is Abbott's."

Joe raised his eyebrows and held out his palms in mock surrender. "Okay, but why didn't you bring this up while we were in there?"

"Because Connie would have kicked us out if we'd asked to search the place. I didn't know what else to do except end the interview."

They stopped at the front door.

"Well, Lou's got the place watched." Joe nodded toward a cruiser parked two doors down. "Let's try again."

Connie didn't open the door so quickly this time. Nor did she invite them in.

"Sam's not back yet," she said as she started to close the door.

Joe put out his hand to block her. "We've got some news we think you'd like to hear."

With a sigh, Connie let them in. "What have you got to tell me?"

Joe moved a few more steps inside. "Only that you turned in the cat to ORA at precisely 5:07 today. We'd like to ask you a few more questions about what happened *after* you took the cat into ORA. We'd also like to talk to your husband. May we come and sit down?"

Connie hesitated. "I suppose." She stepped aside. "Like I said, Sam's not here."

Maureen surveyed the hall leading to the kitchen before moving into the living room. "Still no sign of the cat?"

Connie gave a petulant "No."

Joe began again. "Mrs. Abbott—Connie—take your time to pull your thoughts together. Then, please take us through, step by step, what happened after you took the stray into ORA."

Connie stared, but said nothing.

"Mrs. Abbott, would you mind if I have a quick look around while you collect your thoughts?"

"Go ahead. Look around."

"Thank you."

Joe got up and motioned for Maureen to stay with Connie. The women sat in silence. They could hear Joe searching the main floor and upstairs rooms.

When he returned, he looked at Maureen. She read the disappointment on his face. Nothing.

He turned to Connie. "Most bungalows have a basement. I don't seem to see any stairs to yours."

"Who says we have a basement?"

Maureen got up. "But you do have a garage. May I take a look there?"

"The key is on the hook by the door. But we use it only for storage."

When Maureen drew up the garage door and flicked on a light switch, she looked around and sighed. All she saw was a boat and building and gardening materials.

No cat. No Anastasia.

***

As soon as Maureen left, Connie began speaking in a robotic voice.

"He broke the kitten's leg you know. That's why I had to take her to ORA."

Startled, Joe asked, "Your husband, Sam?"

"Who else?"

"And then what happened, Connie?" Joe prompted.

"I went to ORA. On the way back, I popped into the dollar store across the street to buy a couple of things. At the bus stop I saw a pretty, dark-haired girl waiting for the bus. She wanted to see the cat, but the carrier was empty."

"So what happened?"

"We chatted a bit."

"And?"

"The girl's bus was late. Sam was on his way back up from an electrical supply place near Eastern Avenue and saw us. He said the Queen streetcar was stuck in the intersection at Coxwell, and offered to drive her to the hospital."

"She got into the van with you?" Joe asked.

Connie bowed her head, folded her hands in her lap and said nothing. After a moment, she looked up again, tears welling in her eyes. Then she resumed.

"It all started with Dora Otley—pretty, petite and long dark hair. The way I used to be."

"Tell me about Dora," Joe urged.

"There's nothing much to say. Sam was fixated on her. He incorporated her name into our sex play. Granted, he always liked a bit of kink in our sex. You know, a few little shocks, some slapping and bondage with his cables.

"Then it was kiddie porn." She swallowed hard before continuing. "I didn't expect him to bring home pretty little Caitlyn. Her death was a mistake. Too much electricity." She paused. "You know, I thought we'd just go to the hospital, but Sam had other ideas."

Then Joe felt his phone vibrate in his pocket.

As he dug out his phone, he remembered the surveillance team outside. *Time to call in the cavalry.*

***

Maureen returned to the house through the kitchen's sliding glass door. Once inside, she thought she heard scratching and trilling noises. *Maxie! But where?* She examined the kitchen walls and opened cupboards.

185

As she approached the pantry alcove, the scratching became louder and more frantic. The noise seemed to come from behind a section of empty shelves. She leaned on a ledge to examine it more carefully. To her surprise, the whole unit swung out and a big, furry form scuttled across the floor, heading straight for the kibble bowl. *The missing stairs!* She peered down and saw a dim light below.

She texted Joe and began edging down the steps. She paused halfway and squinted into the dimness. Then she saw a girl with long dark hair tied up and gagged in a corner. *Anastasia!* She started to hurry down, but suddenly someone grabbed her from the side and hurled her to the floor. *Abbott!*

Sam Abbott came at her, flexing a wire cord in his hands. Maureen leapt up, faced him and kicked him in the groin. He staggered back and dropped the cord.

Abbott straightened up and charged at her, growling. Maureen aimed her right elbow at his solar plexus, but Abbott knocked her arm down, spun her around and wrapped her in a bear hug.

Then Joe barreled down the stairs. He trapped Abbott's neck and head in a rear chokehold. Abbott began flailing and released Maureen. Once Abbott stopped struggling, Joe brought him down slowly and flipped him over.

At that point, one of the surveillance officers Joe had summoned raced down the stairs and handcuffed Abbott.

Maureen and Joe knelt and released Anastasia. Though gagged, bound and terrified, she appeared otherwise unhurt. When they went upstairs, they found Connie, under the guard of a second surveillance officer, sitting stoically—one hand clutching the sofa's edge, the other stroking Maxie.

Maxie purred and stared straight ahead.

As Connie was escorted from the house, she looked at Maureen. "Who will take care of Maxie?"

Exasperated, Maureen rolled her eyes, then focused on Connie. "Mrs. Abbott, rest assured Maxie will be fine."

***

About an hour later, as they watched the ambulance take Anastasia and her weeping parents away, Maureen turned to Joe. "It appears you *helped* save my life. Thanks."

A half-smile flickered on Joe's lips. "We all have our moments."

Maureen gave him a poke in the ribs. "But what took you so long?"

Joe cocked his head and raised an eyebrow. With a glint in his eyes and a shrug of his shoulders, he said, "I figured you were on a roll."

About Marilyn Kay

Marilyn Kay debuts two crime short stories this fall: "That Damn Cat" in *13 Claws*, and "Journey into the Dark" in the *Bouchercon Passport to Murder* anthology published in October 2017.

Marilyn began writing as a contributor to the *Dictionary of the Middle Ages*, before working as a business journalist, then in government communications. More recently, she did social media coaching. She is a member of Sisters in Crime and an executive member of Sisters in Crime – Toronto.

You can find her at:
https://marilynkay.me/
https://www.facebook.com/marilynkayauthor/
https://twitter.com/triskeleweb

THE RIGHT CHOICE

By Donna Carrick

There have been times when I've regretted my tendency toward impulsive decision-making.

It's not that I consider myself to be stupid, or rash. I do my best to think things through.

Rather, it's that my process is a quick one by most standards, and involves a great deal of reliance on gut instinct.

For the most part, my gut has served me well.

I lifted a photo from the shelf and smiled into the faces of my husband, Gerald, and our only son, Hal.

I'd fallen in love with Gerald almost instantly. Certainly, by our second date, I was committed, and it was only a matter of waiting for his feelings to catch up with mine.

Was it the right decision on my part?

I smiled again and dusted the frame with my sleeve before putting it in its place.

Without a doubt, marrying Gerald was the best thing I'd ever done. It was followed a year later by the birth of our wonderful son.

But I can't claim that every one of my personal choices was a winner. Oh, no, not by a long shot!

I've been lucky, more or less, but a time or two my instincts led me dangerously astray.

When I first met Gerald, I was firmly on the rebound from one such unfortunate decision.

Stephen.

That was his name.

Blue eyes flashing under a mop of angel-blond hair.

A smile that could explode into laughter without warning, carrying everyone around him into a state of pure mirth.

Or, equally without warning, sour into a frown, erupt in anger.

Words that would knock you down…a fist that could make sure you stayed down…

That was Stephen.

It didn't take me long to admit my mistake in loving Stephen.

It took him a lot longer to accept my decision to leave.

The restraining order didn't do the job. He continued to follow me, to come around day or night.

When I called the police, he became more subtle in his approach, more sly.

I couldn't prove it, but I knew he'd been in my apartment many times during the six months after our break-up.

My father, God rest his soul, stepped into the mess and put an end to it.

"Stay away from Angela," he said simply.

His words were punctuated by the boot he'd placed on Stephen's throat, and the guns he and his two fellow officers pointed at my ex.

***

I stepped into the kitchen, humming "All My Ex's Live in Texas."

Daisy roused herself and followed me, looking for breakfast.

Bringing Daisy home as a pup had been another snap decision, and one that still brought a smile to my face all these years later.

I remembered the day I'd chosen her from a litter of irresistible golden retriever pups. They looked like overgrown hamsters, wobbling around on uncertain legs, just beginning to discover the art of play.

Hal was two years old at the time. Both Gerald and I had grown up with dogs, so deciding to have one in the house was easy.

We had agreed on a golden, since we knew the breed to be especially gentle with young children. Of course, at the time, we didn't know Hal would be our only child. We envisioned a house filled with youngsters, and our Daisy acting as a stand in for Nana, the nursemaid dog of the Darling household in *Peter Pan*.

There were six pups in the litter, an even split between male and female.

One gorgeous little boy pup bounced over to Gerald, who was taken with his energy immediately.

But it was Daisy, the smallest of the lot, who nudged Hal with her nose and made him laugh.

It was Daisy, a puffy ball of fur, who navigated her way onto Hal's lap and struggled to reach his chin for a slobbery kiss.

My mind was made up.

Daisy was ours.

No regrets, that's for sure.

She'd grown up so fine, so stately over the years. In no time, we could hardly recall the sweet little runt who'd stolen our hearts.

Daisy was a queen among dogs, proud head, magnificent in her bearing, stunning in her beauty.

A dog with a sense of humor, quick to break into a furry grin when her people told a joke or paid special attention to her.

For the next four years, right up until the day I lost Gerald and Hal in a terrible hit-and-run, Daisy was the light of our lives.

She worshipped Hal, following him everywhere, and when he went off to kindergarten, her eyes would repeatedly find the door, waiting and hoping for his return.

When my father died last year, cancer consuming his lungs less than a year after his retirement from the force, it was Daisy who gave me the strength to carry on.

Her loving face, her persistent care sustained me. During the worst of my grief, when I found it impossible to get out of bed, she would lie next to me, barely moving, never asking for her food, waiting with enduring patience to be walked, to be fed.

It was caring for her that got me through each day.

I reached into the cupboard for her bag of kibble.

She was an old girl. More than 12 years, a good age for a golden. Despite a measure of slowness to her gait, she was in excellent shape. I credited our long walks and her enthusiasm for life for keeping her healthy.

As she crunched on the smelly kernels, my eyes landed on my Keurig. Time for coffee.

I opened the cupboard over the sink and reached for a mug.

Without looking I pulled out my favorite cup. Then, before I could place it onto the counter, my hand froze in midair.

Something wasn't right!

I studied the mug in horror.

The mug in my hand was *not* my favorite. Also, I have a lifelong habit of putting the cups away upside down, turned over to avoid collecting dust.

One look into the cupboard was all I needed to be sure.

Three of my cups had been tampered with—turned upside right and moved around, so that my favorite one was set behind the others.

Let me be clear.

Except for Daisy, I live alone.

My father, who had a habit of dropping by without warning, has been gone to that great donut shop in the sky for the better part of a year.

As smart as she was, Daisy never learned to wash and dry dishes.

As for me, my habits are fairly well-formed.

Anyone else would say I was losing my mind, but I recognized this for what it was: Stephen was back in my life.

He must have heard of Dad's passing.

For whatever reason, he was back.

I returned Gerald's old unused mug to the cupboard—upside down, thank you very much—and turned the others over before removing my own mug and placing it onto the counter.

With Daisy at my side, I double-checked the locks on every window and door in my modest home before setting the java to brew.

When had he been here?

It must have been within the past 24 hours.

As I said, my habits are consistent. I brew a cup every morning at precisely this time before taking Daisy out for her walk.

Then it's off to work for eight hours, returning home in time to take Daisy out to the local park before dark.

We usually walk and play catch for about an hour. That must be when Stephen broke into the house.

How long had he been watching me, stalking, studying my movements, before he figured out it was just me and Daisy now?

A gentler, less threatening pooch you'd never meet.

Still, even the most passive of dogs will protect its home, so no doubt Stephen had waited till our evening walk before trespassing.

Who knows? Maybe he'd never stopped watching me. Maybe he was well aware of those happy years, when Gerald and I laughed and shared the joy of watching our baby grow into a school-aged boy.

Maybe Stephen had been there all along, breathing heavily on the fringes of my life, waiting for his chance to carry out the threats of long ago.

***

It was Saturday morning, and a fine one at that. After letting Daisy into the yard for a moment, I carried my coffee to the deck. She *harrumphed* and dropped at my feet, laying her snout onto folded front paws. She looked at me, raising first one eyebrow, then the other, in that comical way of hers, until I laughed at last and relaxed into the morning.

What the hell? I knew Dad still had friends on the force who would be only too happy to help his daughter.

There was Fred O'Leary, a fifty-something health fanatic who'd had a massive heart attack three years earlier, but had recovered sufficiently to resume duties, albeit on desk work.

And Ricky Stromm, who was maybe 10 years younger than Fred, and who had been the one to stand beside me at Dad's funeral, keeping me steady on my feet as the last of my world came crashing down.

Either of them would jump at the chance to have a word with my unruly ex.

But it was Saturday morning, and too early to be calling old friends, waking them from a weekend sleep.

I sipped my hot drink and fiddled with my phone, placing a bud in each ear and finding my favorite news channel.

Nazis and white supremacists were marching with the KKK in Somewheresville—as usual the news was anything but good. I listened for a moment before switching to the music app.

"Come on, girl," I said, rising to my feet.

I stroked her head and mane, remembering those better days, when mornings were perfection, when Gerald and Hal would gather at the breakfast table, teasing me and each other and laughing, their mouths full of Saturday morning eggs and bacon, strawberry jam on their chins, and a much younger Daisy prancing around the table in delight, hoping for a crumb to fall her way.

I let out a sigh. The days and nights of sorrow were over now. I seldom indulged in crying anymore, instead allowing my good memories to carry me forward, determined to find a new purpose, a new reason to live.

Daisy kept me alive, forcing me to put one good foot in front of the other.

Time for our walk.

***

The park was teeming with joggers and fellow dog-walkers, all the early morning folk who, like me, cherish this slice of each new day.

I knew many of them by sight, though only a few by name.

A number of people nodded and waved in passing. Daisy was beyond the days of chasing other canine friends. She merely wagged her tail as they inspected her, slowing our walk but not interrupting it.

As usual, I kept a single treat in my pocket. She knew it was there, but paid it no attention. Once we were ready to leave the park, I would give it to her.

It was such a fine morning that I almost forgot about the mystery of the coffee mugs.

Almost.

I checked the time. Still too early to make a call.

After we returned home, I'd take a second coffee onto the deck and reach out to Fred and Ricky.

They'd know exactly what to do.

***

Daisy and I found an empty bench. Making ourselves comfortable, we watched the movement of humans and canines passing by. I reached into one pocket for her treat, and into the other for my phone.

I'd kept tabs on Stephen over the years, careful not to leave a cyber footprint. Careful not to invite him into my sphere by tapping too firmly into the cosmos.

For instance, I knew when, two years after our calamitous break up, he'd married Cindy, the sweet school teacher. I knew through Dad's friends on the force when, a year later, he was arrested on domestic violence charges.

And shortly after his divorce was final, he entered his second marriage, this time to a Filipino woman by the name of Theresa.

Theresa, bless her heart, stood by her man longer than either Cindy or I had, refusing to press charges after a case of battery that was brutal enough to make the evening news.

That marriage lasted three years, before Theresa finally got the message and fled back to the Philippines.

She discovered what Cindy and I already knew: loving Stephen was one truly bad decision.

I was grateful, despite my losses, for the blessings I'd enjoyed.

I'd known what it meant to have a family. A good, strong father who raised me after my mother died...a husband who never failed to hold my hand in public...a son who filled our home with laughter and light...

And, of course, our Daisy.

Yes, I'd made a lot of good choices in my life, choices that were easy to defend, choices that others could and did envy.

But there was no denying it: I'd taken at least one exceedingly wrong turn.

Stephen.

***

Daisy and I made our way reluctantly back to the empty house.

Having never been a "joiner," I had nothing on the agenda for the weekend.

By the time my coffee was ready, it would be late enough to justify making a call or two.

I fumbled for my key, holding the lead in my left hand as I used my right to unlock the front door.

I won't pretend we had any instinctive reaction, either Daisy or myself.

I won't pretend our Spidey senses kicked in, or that the hair stood up at the backs of our necks.

No.

Neither of us had the slightest notion that we were not alone.

I removed her lead and she trotted into the kitchen to make sure she'd cleaned her breakfast bowl. I followed, with coffee and Cheerios on my mind.

***

"Hello, Angela."

I jumped, startled by the familiar voice.

Daisy growled, slinking to my side, pressing her body against my leg.

"How's it going?"

"What are you doing here, Stephen?"

"I think you know." He smiled, but it wasn't the winning, charming smile of his youth, the smile that lured you into believing he was normal.

This smile was an evil mask, oozing ill intent from the upturned corners of his mouth.

He lifted his hand, showing me the blade of a hunting knife, the same one I'd once found hidden in the linen cupboard of our apartment.

My mind raced. *Best to show no fear. Best to keep it normal, keep it civil.*

"I was about to brew coffee. Would you like a cup?" I smiled and pulled two fresh mugs from the cupboard, ignoring the fact they had once again been turned right-side up.

"Sorry to hear about your father." He turned that malicious smile my way. "Martin was a good man, a good cop."

"Thank you," I said, deliberately ignoring the underlying malevolence in his voice.

"How long has it been since the accident?"

He meant the day my husband and our child had been killed, driving back from Pickering. It had happened during the pre-dawn hours of a Saturday morning.

A terrible hit-and-run that sent our minivan spiralling into the dividers and bouncing back into oncoming traffic, causing a deadly collision that could have been much worse, if the hour had been later, and if traffic had begun to build to its normal level.

A horrible accident that killed Gerald immediately and sent Hal into a coma for a week before robbing him of his young life.

We'd left Daisy at home, and wanted to get back in time to walk her, that's why we were on the road so early.

The mystery of the unknown "other driver" had never been solved. Witnesses said his plate had been removed, and his silver RV could have been one of thousands of its model in the Toronto area.

"I asked how long it's been," he repeated, "since Gerald and Hal were killed?"

I stiffened. *How dare he utter their names? How dare he soil their memory with his foul voice?*

I regained my composure before placing the coffee mug in front of him on the counter.

"Eight years," I said, then added as an afterthought, "today."

"That's what I thought."

"Why do you ask?" I struggled for a neutral tone.

"How did it feel losing everything?"

I stroked Daisy's shoulder, noting the tension in her muscle. *Not quite everything,* I thought.

As usual, he was talking *at* me, not really interested in hearing my answer.

"Sorry about the kid," he continued. "That was a mistake."

I braced myself against the counter, very much aware that Stephen stood between me and possible escape. Daisy remained alert, her body quivering against my leg.

Holding my mug in my left hand, I reached behind me with my right, quietly opening the drawer beside the sink, the one containing old receipts and clean dish towels.

"Are you saying it was you, Stephen? Did you cause the accident?"

I wanted to scream, to throw myself at him, to call him a murderer, but I remained as calm as possible, knowing why he'd come, today of all days, and hoping to stall his act of violence.

"I followed you to Pickering the night before it happened. I watched you laughing, watched you holding hands with him and with your kid. I parked across the street and waited. I thought you'd have dinner, then leave, but you stayed overnight." He paused, searching my face to be sure I understood what he had done. "We were supposed to be married. You were supposed to hold my hand, have my kid. We were supposed to be a family."

"Stephen," I said, "that was a long time ago. You've been married since then."

He nodded. "Twice."

"Then why are you here? Why are you still watching me, after all these years?"

"I never stopped. I've always been here, watching you. After the accident I thought you'd call me. I thought you'd reach out, let me comfort you."

A slow rage bubbled in my craw, but I swallowed it.

"But you'd moved on," I said. "You'd made another life for yourself. You didn't need me anymore."

It was the wrong thing to say. I watched as his smiling mask dissolved into fury.

Daisy sensed it, too. She tensed beside me, crouching ever so slightly.

That was all the warning we were given. A change of face, a sudden cloud covering the sun.

Stephen lunged, knocking over his coffee cup, the knife held firmly in his raised fist.

Daisy sprang, catching him off balance and causing him to step back slightly.

In a flash, he righted himself, plunging the hunting knife deep into her throat.

Her cream-colored fur became stained with a gruesome shade of red.

It was over in an instant. There was no time to think, no time to run before he was once again coming at me with the knife.

"You should have died that day. Why didn't you die?"

There was no time to think, but, thanks to Daisy's final act, there had been time to put my hand onto Dad's old service revolver, the one I kept fully loaded, hidden under the old receipts and clean dishcloths, in the kitchen drawer beside the sink.

I lifted my hand and fired, point blank, into the face of evil.

Stepping around Stephen's body, and carefully passing Daisy, who was dead on the floor, I carried my coffee onto the deck.

I pulled my phone from my pocket and scrolled through my contacts to *O'Leary*.

"Fred," I said when he answered, "I need your help. Can you and Ricky come over, right away?"

Then I dialed 9-1-1.

***

First responders arrived only moments before my father's old buddies pulled up to the curb. Fred O'Leary and Ricky Stromm remained at my side throughout the questioning process, and waited patiently while I was questioned by police.

Stephen was pronounced dead. My father's weapon was taken into evidence, as was the hunting knife Stephen had used to slaughter Daisy.

I gave a statement at the division while the forensics team and cleanup squad finished their work at the house.

I wasn't sure I'd ever find a way to scour my mind, to clear the memory of that morning.

***

By late afternoon, I was home again, on my own.

This time, though, *alone* really *meant* alone. There was no Daisy to help me overcome the shock, the grief.

With a fresh cup of coffee, I curled up on the couch, too exhausted for sleep, thinking of all the choices, good and bad, I'd made during the course of my lifetime.

Gerald and Hal were the two best decisions I've ever made. Even knowing the pain of their loss, I'd still trust my gut and do it all again. I'd give anything for another day, another hour with them.

Stephen had been a mistake from the start. It hadn't taken long to see what a bastard he was, how dangerous and how volatile.

But Daisy…Daisy…Daisy… What could I say about our dear Daisy?

Runt of the litter, soul of a lion.

Daisy was, without a doubt, the right choice.

About Donna Carrick

Donna is the author of 3 crime novels: *The First Excellence ~ Fa ling's Map*; *The Noon God*; *Gold And Fishes*.

In addition, Donna has authored three short story collections: *North on the Yellowhead*; *Knowing Penelope*; *Sept-Îles and Other Places*. She is also a contributing author for several anthologies, including: *World Enough and Crime*; *13 O'Clock*; *EFD1 – Starship Goodwords*; *Thirteen*.

Donna served on the board of Crime Writers of Canada for six years as treasurer, and volunteered as a mentor for new author members.

When not writing, Donna co-owns and operates the Indie publishing house Carrick Publishing, with her husband Alex Carrick.

Connect with Donna at:

donnacarrick.com and at carrickpublishing.com

Facebook: Donna Carrick, Carrick Publishing and the group Excerpt Flight Deck for Readers and Authors

Twitter: @Donna_Carrick and @CarrickPub

LinkedIn: linkedin.com/in/donnacarrick/

Goodreads.com/author/show/65922.Donna_Carrick

Or at MesdamesofMayhem.com

ANIMAL CRACKERS

By Catherine Dunphy

Winona couldn't see the sad in the shabby. All she could see was that there were too many of them taking up too many seats at the library this winter.

They cowered behind stacks of books, sometimes not even shrugging off their winter coats. There were days when the library was so warm and toasty that Winona would prance down its aisles and stacks in one of her cherished sleeveless cotton shirts with the embroidered Chinese collars favored in the 1950s, her go-to decade.

She let out a long sigh. Furtive, she thought to herself, they look furtive. Take the trio who had just scuttled off to the far corner, heads ducked into upturned frayed coat collars. All she had said was "Good morning" but they'd reacted as if assaulted.

Last night, Jason had accused her of being elitist, of not accepting that in cold weather the library was a refuge for the homeless men locked out of the town hostel until suppertime. Okay, so they had no interest in books, or reading, or learning; okay, so they took up space that others could have used. Okay, so they had no use of Winona's librarian talents or Internet search skills.

"Win, they know that they don't belong. Even in a *public*—" he'd loaded the word with irony "—library."

Okay, so he had a point. Winona's live-in boyfriend was a Sanderson Taylor, the scion of the town's leading family. But he had a big, bleeding heart and pretty good instincts for people, as well. She should chill and get back to work. Yes, that's exactly what she would do.

She was deep into the library's treasure trove of fan-friendly websites—her own initiative—when a pale yellow blur confronted her.

A very agitated man was waving a package of Barnum's Animal Crackers in her face.

She sighed. "We don't allow food in the library. Sorry."

But she wasn't sorry at all. For one thing, she was a size 18, and food was the last thing she needed in her workplace. For another, it was still a library, for God's sake. She went back to her screen.

The man heaved a sigh that matched her own, making Winona look up again.

"Please," he said. "I need to know where to get the other kind."

"Try the grocery store."

He winced, and she felt terrible. She knew she'd been cranky lately—about everything. She knew there was no logical reason why. Her life was fine. Good job. Great guy at home. Good stuff on Netflix most nights, too.

Time to apologize. "Forgive me, I shouldn't have—"

A tear was rolling down the man's weathered cheek.

"Oh my God." She said it so loudly that one of the three guys in the corner peered over his stack of books. Winona grabbed an empty chair from the nearest reading table and pulled it toward her desk. It scraped along the wooden floor with a great screech. She resisted the urge to give the finger to the lady by the fireplace, who signaled her displeasure by rattling the pages of her newspaper.

"Please. Please sit down."

His face was kind. He looked as if he had laughed a lot at one time. He took off and carefully folded his coat on his lap. His collared shirt under his dark blue V-necked sweater was clean and pressed, but open to reveal the hollows of age round his neck. Somebody's grandfather, she thought.

She watched him place this ordinary cookie package on the desk between them. Somebody's addled grandfather, she amended.

"When I was a boy, they used to have these in little boxes. Not like these packages. Shaped like circus wagons. String on top. The wheels folded down. All the kids loved them. They still do, right?" He leaned toward her and tapped the back of her computer. "Can you find them in there?"

Winona cocked an eyebrow. Could she? This was just the kind of search she lived for. And if—no, when—she located those funky crackers, she'd order some for herself. She held up a finger signaling the man to wait and then dived into her favourite world. First, get past the Walmart links. Then she sat back. Interesting.

She turned the screen so that the man could see too.

"The first animal crackers were made in York, Pennsylvania in 1871 by Stauffer's. They're still making them. Whoa! To the tune of 250 tons of animal crackers a day." She scanned the website. "They've got orange whales and frosted ones and ginger—hey, lemon too."

She stopped. The man was agitated, waving his package of cookies. "No, no, no. That's this kind. They're not special. That won't make him happy."

Winona swung the screen back and clicked a couple more times. "Here."

He gasped. On the screen was the old-fashioned red-and-yellow box of Barnum's Animal Crackers. The string on top. The cut-out wheels. The gorilla, hippo, monkey and lion in circus cages. "That's it."

Winona read through the copy. "By 1902, animal crackers were being made by the National Biscuit Company in the States, which later became Nabisco, and were called Barnum's Animals. That year, the company designed a box for the Christmas season with the innovative idea of attaching a string to hang the boxes from Christmas trees. They sold for a nickel a box."

Winona whooped, forgetting herself and her surroundings. "Until that time, crackers had been generally only sold in bulk—thus the phrase *cracker barrel*," she read out. "How cool is that?" she asked.

But the man was kneading the package of cookies, frowning and rocking on his chair. "They're not in any stores here. I need to buy them. There's this boy—"

She stopped herself from putting a comforting hand on the man. He was visibly upset. "You can order them on the Internet."

He leapt up. "No, I can't." It was a howl, and it was heard in every corner of the reading room. One of the homeless guys looked up, got to his feet and crossed the library surprisingly fast.

"You're disturbing things, Johnny," he said. Winona got a good look at him. His sand- coloured hair needed washing, but his puffy winter jacket was neither grimy nor even much worn, and his blue eyes were clear. He gripped the older man's forearm and led him out of the library. Winona rocked back in her chair, staring after them, wondering.

***

"Of course he can't get them himself," Jason snapped at her. Snapped! Jason! At her!

Winona watched warily as her boyfriend rearranged his long legs under the kitchen table and sat up straighter on his chair, readying for some major pronouncement. If he broke up with her over animal crackers—

"I am losing you to this." He tapped the laptop, which was open in front of her. "Not everyone is like you. Not everyone lives online. That old guy. You think he has a PayPal account? A credit card? An address?"

Winona started to reply, but something in his face stopped her. He looked so sad.

"You are forgetting the real world, Win," he said, getting up from the table. "Millartown. Right here."

The sounds of a hockey game were blaring on the living room television when Winona finally fired up her computer and ordered three boxes of Barnum's Animal Crackers.

Relations were still a little strained between Jason and her when they were delivered a week later just before she was to leave for her shift. She was on afternoons all week.

She showed him the package. "See. I did hear you."

Jason frowned. "No, you didn't." He loped out of the room.

"I did, too." Winona shrieked, waving the delivery package after him, rattling its contents. Damn, she probably broke a few. She had no idea why Jason was still in a snit, but somehow she was going to give that sad and sweet old man his Animal Crackers.

***

The library was overrun with strollers and streaking toddlers. Winona hung up her felt appliquéd coat, stashed her cuffed winter boots in the staff cubby and squared her shoulders. She'd worn her favorite pencil skirt with a cardigan sweater buttoned backward. She figured she needed to look great to cope with the twice-weekly moms-and-tots sessions that took every bit of her patience. She loathed the school-aged reading groups even more. The other librarians were happy to lead those groups, handing off their research duties to Winona, who was grateful to be able to bury herself in the Internet.

Oh. Winona stood stock-still. Is this what Jason meant?

She marched over to the corner table where she knew the men from the hostel would be, dozing behind their book wall. She was in luck. The man with the blue gaze from last week was back. He looked up from the Carl Sagan book he was reading as she thrust the package at him. "For Johnny." Of course she remembered the old man's name.

He closed his book, but not before inserting one of the library's bookmarks to hold his spot—Winona couldn't help but be impressed. He opened the package; his features hardened when he saw the cookies.

"You have no idea what you are doing, do you?"

Winona rocked back on her heels.

"These are the ones he wanted." She jabbed at the package. Damn it! First Jason, now him.

He stood up and leaned towards Winona. "Forget he ever told you about this, you hear me?" He stared right into her eyes, frightening her. "Forget you ever saw him. And get rid of those."

Grabbing his coat from the back of the chair, he didn't wait for his companion but strode straight for the door. Winona had instinctively and protectively grabbed the package when he suddenly turned on his heels and crossed back to her in a couple of strides. "It's for your own good," he said very quietly. Then he was gone.

Winona dropped into the seat he'd just vacated. His friend jumped to his feet.

"Please don't go," she said.

He glanced beyond her but waited.

"You know Johnny? Where I can find him?" Winona asked.

He hesitated. He was a small man, the kind who keeps to corners, taking comfort in the background.

"Johnny don't come here no more," he said finally. "But he don't know that." He jerked his head in the direction where his blue-eyed companion had gone.

Winona didn't care what that man knew or didn't know. "But Johnny, he's still sleeping at the hostel?"

A nod.

Good enough, Winona thought. She'd go to the hostel tomorrow morning before everyone left for the day. Find Johnny and suss out the story behind these crackers he was so desperate for.

"Miss?" The man's voice cracked as if from disuse. "That Johnny. I don't know, miss. There's something—"

He shoved a wool cap on his uncombed head. "Be careful."

"Of what?" Winona wanted to scream as she watched him amble out into the cold.

***

But when she finally arrived at the hostel—mornings were never her best time—only a small group of men were still there, huddled against the day's wind, discolored hands shielding the embers of their cigarettes. They were more interested in bumming more fags than in giving her info about Johnny.

"Who? That strange one?" a man said. "The guy's damn jumpy."

"Done some time, for sure." This guy looked like he would know.

The first man spoke again. "He's got something going on, that one."

He pointed west, toward the part of town where families were reclaiming streets of tired, small semidetached homes. "He always goes off that way."

Not knowing what else to do, Winona trudged in the direction he'd indicated. The street wasn't a busy one except for the school at its end. The kids were tearing around the playground for the last few minutes before the morning bell summoned them inside. She thought it might be one of Millartown's older schools. Maybe one of its better ones. Not that she'd know.

As she stood there, a teacher came out, blew a whistle and hustled the kids inside. She looked across the playground right at Winona. Not friendly. The woman gave a start and reached for her phone. Behind her, Winona heard somebody scrambling to leave. *Johnny!*

"Wait." She grabbed at his coat sleeve.

"No. They'll get me." Johnny pushed her away with surprising strength.

Winona ran after him. "I've got your crackers, damn it," she shouted.

He stopped, looking around wildly. "Not here. Not here."

Winona followed him to a faded coffee shop. The waitress—middle-aged, Greek and probably the owner— slammed thick white cups onto saucers, dropped a couple of creamers onto the Formica tabletop and poured scalding coffee from a great height.

She didn't spill a drop.

Winona tipped a stream of sugar into her coffee.

The man called Johnny stared at the package on the table between them. Winona was taken aback when he asked her permission to open it, which he then did with careful precision. He lined up the three boxes in front of him and smiled at her. Winona's heart was moved.

"All kids still love them, right? They're still special, right?"

"Right," she replied. And then she couldn't help herself. "Who's the lucky kid?"

"Noah. He's my—" He hurriedly stashed the packages into his duffel bag and stood up. He shoved a grimy $10 bill across the table at her. "You're a nice lady. Thank you."

And that was that, Winona thought as she slowly sipped her sweet beverage and thought about things. About why she was suddenly taking a pound of sugar in her coffee these days. And why Johnny was so frightened.

She started. The man from the library, the one with the strong blue gaze, was sitting across from her in Johnny's place. She had heard nothing; the air had scarcely moved to signal his presence.

"Who the hell are you anyway?" Her voice was so loud that a couple of the other customers looked over.

He ignored her question. "You are going to tell me what you've got going with the old guy."

Winona thought of Johnny and his smile, and she wasn't afraid. "Nope. I'm not."

Suddenly he grabbed Winona's arm. "What did you give him?"

"Refill?" It was the waitress. She lifted the pot of coffee high and poured right onto his hand.

"Fuck," he barked.

The waitress apologized and blocked his way as she dabbed at his arm with paper napkins. Winona fled.

She was gasping from fear as much as exertion when she flung open the door to her apartment. She needed Jason.

Thankfully, he hadn't yet left for his part-time shift at the library. She sat down beside him. "I am trying to get into the real world, Jason. For you," she said. "But it's scaring me."

He took her hand, and she told him everything.

***

The next morning, Winona defiantly threw her prized fox-head wrap over her vintage tweed coat, and she and Jason walked to the schoolyard. They stood across the street and watched a slight figure in a shabby jacket cross the yard and approach one of the smaller boys standing off by himself. They watched Johnny hand the boy the package; the boy looked up at him and smiled. They watched the boy leap into Johnny's arms, hugging him fiercely. They watched Johnny bend his head, his grizzled cheek brushing the top of the boy's dark hair. They watched the two lock together as if they were a pair of puzzle pieces.

Then a burly blur was charging toward Johnny and Noah, screaming profanities. He was as powerful as he was fast, grabbing the boy, jerking him apart from Johnny. The boy screamed in terror. Johnny stumbled backward as the man pulled him by the collar and pummelled him with huge fists. The brass knuckles on his right hand caught the sun as he struck—again and again. Not stopping when Johnny collapsed onto the ground, not stopping when Johnny's arms, raised in a futile attempt to ward off the blows, dropped lifeless to his sides.

Winona gasped. Beside her, she could feel Jason tense and lean forward, about to help. "He's going to kill that old guy," Jason said.

Then the sandy-haired man with the blue gaze streaked across the schoolyard. In two swift moves he had Noah and was hustling the boy toward the school. The boy let out a wail. Jason put out a protective arm as Winona started forward.

"Cops," he said. "Look."

Two police cruisers screamed around the corner, sirens shrieking and lights blazing. They skidded to a halt half on the sidewalk. Four uniformed officers raced towards the playground. Some of the kids broke into cheers, others were rooted in awe. Worried staff poured out of the school, herding everyone inside. One of them wrapped Noah in her arms and hustled him away.

Winona exhaled. Noah was safe. Johnny would be rescued.

It took three policemen to pull Johnny's attacker off him. The screaming man writhed and kicked at them with his steel-toed boots, his dark eyes wild and his thin mouth a snarl. The cops tackled him to the ground and snapped a pair of cuffs on him. Still, he bucked and fought, screaming, "You assholes. Get him. Him. Not me."

Then, to Winona's horror, the other police officer helped Johnny to his feet only to clamp a pair of cufflinks on him, too.

Tears ran down Winona's face, blurring everything as Johnny was led to the police cruiser.

Then the man with the blue gaze was in front of her again, proffering his badge.

Anger and disgust spilled out from Winona. "Why are you taking Johnny? That's his grandson. You do know that, right?"

The plainclothes cop was quiet for a moment.

"Johnny's just got out after serving four years for aggravated assault," he said, unconsciously rubbing the reddened part of his hand where the waitress had poured the hot coffee.

Winona gasped. "Assault? Johnny?"

"He cut up his son-in-law pretty bad." The cop looked back at the schoolyard, and Winona suddenly understood.

"That animal was Noah's father?"

The cop frowned. "He accused Johnny of messing with a minor. Told him he was going to turn him in. They were in the kitchen. Johnny grabbed the nearest knife."

Winona reeled and leaned against Jason for support.

"Noah?" The name came out in a whisper.

"I am not at liberty to confirm that identity," the cop said. But he nodded. "That part never came to trial. Johnny wouldn't let his defense use it. Cost him the verdict, if you ask me."

A harsh fall wind suddenly rushed around them. The cop shivered and sank deeper into his jacket.

"Everyone we talked to said Johnny lived for the boy, took care—good care—of him from the time he was in diapers. Somebody had to."

Winona frowned. "Then why—"

The cop cut her off. "I'll be straight with you. But you say one word to anyone else, and I'll deny everything. Clear?"

Winona and Jason exchanged looks and nodded.

"The son–in-law's not Noah's dad. If you ask me, that's probably for the best. His name is Brandon Gleen, and he's got a real bad temper. Works at playing the ponies. Never wins. Pays off his debts helping his bookie collect from other deadbeats. You see the hardware on his hand?"

Winona was horrified. That poor little kid, living with a man like that. He must go to bed at night so very frightened.

The cop seemed to be reading her mind. "Noah's mother—Johnny's daughter—thinks the sun rises and sets because of him. Been beholden to Gleen since he moved in with them when Noah was still in diapers. When he made it clear he was doing her a favor letting her keep the kid."

Winona's heart was sinking.

"But why arrest Johnny now? He was just trying to give his grandson a gift."

"Yeah. Why the sirens and cuffs?" Jason added.

"The day before Johnny walked free, Gleen was in court getting a restraining order. Johnny can't go near the boy."

The cop looked at Winona. "Been tailing Johnny waiting for Gleen to strike. Word on the street was Gleen couldn't wait to inflict some payback on him. When you gave Johnny those cookies, we knew he was going to try and see the kid right away. I get why. Probably Johnny wanted to see for himself that Noah was okay. Not hurt any by Gleen."

He shook his head. "But we also figured Gleen would strike soon. Not give Johnny a chance to reconnect with the kid. And we were pretty sure he'd do his dirty work in front of the boy. That's the kind of gentleman he is."

Winona was dumbfounded. She felt Jason tighten his grip on her hand.

"So stuff like this doesn't just happen in thrillers," she whispered.

"Nope. We'll push for aggravated assault charges against Gleen. He should get sent down for four long years, just like Johnny." The cop grinned, but his eyes were serious. "Gleen won't be going home any time soon. Noah will be safe now."

"But Johnny's not there for him," Winona practically wailed.

The man shrugged. "He may get off with a warning, but I know what you're thinking and no, it's not fair."

He turned away, then stopped. "Some days I hate my job."

Winona wiped her eyes with her sleeve. The schoolyard was empty save for the three boxes of animal crackers on the ground, flashing their cheerful primary colors. Jason followed her as she picked up the packages, stuffed them back in her carrier bag. They trudged home in silence.

***

The next morning, Winona and Jason slipped out of the apartment before breakfast. Neither had slept much the previous night, and at some point before dawn, Winona had decided to return to the school. After yesterday's action, she wasn't sure if they'd even be allowed into the building; true to her misgivings, when she pushed open the door to the principal's office, the matronly school secretary frowned at her over the rim of her glasses.

Then she broke into a big smile.

"Winona, what brings you here?"

It was the president of Winona's fan fiction group. She couldn't believe her luck.

Before she could answer the woman put her finger to her lips. The voice of the principal filled the office and spread throughout the school making the announcements of the day.

Winona looked about her. The mark of the students was everywhere. Cheerful posters of an upcoming FUN Fair. Warnings about never being a bully.

A cheap but gleaming trophy was on display beside a color photo of the track team, everyone proud and grinning. Winona moved across the room to peer at it. Yes, he was there. Noah. Second row, fourth from the left, looking happily at the camera.

When the announcements ended, Winona beckoned to the secretary. Winona pointed to Noah in the picture and thrust the bag with the crackers at her. "These are for Noah. Please make sure he gets these. Please. Noah loves them."

The secretary studied Winona. No fool, she checked that the boxes were unopened, had not been tampered with. Her face softened. "I remember these."

Back outside, Jason took her arm. "You're doing good in the real world."

***

A week later, Winona was back at the school. It was the midmorning recess, and this time Noah was surrounded by a small circle of kids his size. Very excited kids. He was showing off his animal crackers.

So this is the world of children, she thought to herself. Maybe it's not so bad after all.

Winona smiled and looked down at her tummy.

About Catherine Dunphy

A National Newspaper Award winner for feature writing, Catherine Dunphy was a staff writer at *The Toronto Star*, Canada's largest newspaper, for more than 25 years.

She is the author of *Morgentaler, A Difficult Hero*, which was nominated for the prestigious Governor General's Award in 1997. As well, she has written two books of young adult fiction related to the much-heralded Canadian television series, *Degrassi High*, which has been shown throughout the world.

She has also written screenplays for the Canadian television series, *Riverdale*, as well as created a four-part *CBC* radio mystery series called *Fallaway Ridge*. She continues to write for magazines and is at work on a literary novel. She has always been a mystery reader/addict.

SNAKEBIT

By Ed Piwowarczyk

Jake Turner studied the blonde as she entered The Hideaway. Her denim shorts highlighted shapely legs, and a white tank top accented perky breasts. A sexy package, he thought.

With my luck, she's probably trouble with a capital T.

Turner watched as the woman ran a hand through her short, slightly tousled hair and surveyed the bar. Its walls were adorned with sports memorabilia, celebrity photos, beer signs and rock concert posters from the sixties and seventies—glory days for Steelsboro before the city had become a notch in America's Rust Belt. The Hideaway was a down-at-the-heels shrine to those days gone by, and its patrons were workers from neighboring factories and warehouses. Turner had chosen their blue-collar uniform—jeans, black T-shirt, denim vest—to blend in with his surroundings.

Yesterday, the bartender, Steve, had told him, a woman had come in, put a couple of coins in the Wurlitzer on the back wall, punched in a few songs, and asked for The Snake. Not here, don't know when he'll be around, Steve had said.

"I'll leave a message anyway," she'd said. "Tell The Snake to be here tomorrow. And tell him to play B12 if he wants to do business."

Turner's antennae had gone up, but he needed to "do business" badly. He had only two more days to pay off his gambling debts to the Mob.

He gave Steve a quizzical look. *Is this her?*

Steve nodded.

Turner slid his six-foot-two-inch frame off the bar stool and strode over to the jukebox to punch in B12. The blonde was poised to leave, but turned around and began to sway as The Zombies' "She's Not There" pulsed through the Wurlitzer's speakers.

Half a dozen midafternoon regulars studied her as she strolled to the jukebox, fished some change out of a blue leather tote bag and punched in more picks. Turner picked up two cans of beer and two glasses, and motioned her to a booth in the back.

"So I finally meet The Snake." She sat down across from him and poured herself a glass of beer.

He took a drink. "And you're…?"

"Mercedes, but most people call me Sadie."

"How did you hear about me?"

"Let's just say I'm…connected."

Her sapphire eyes flicked to his right forearm. "That why they call you The Snake? Fast and deadly?"

He glanced down at his tattoo—a diamondback rattlesnake with an oversized head, fangs bared, coiled and ready to strike. He nodded. "You don't want to mess with me."

She smiled, then studied him. "Ex-military?"

"Uh-huh."

"I grew up as a military brat, so I can sense it." She swallowed some beer. "A little too old for the field?"

"I'm not as old as you think." He was pushing 50, but he prided himself on maintaining a ripped physique.

Sadie nodded. "All right, time to talk business." Her smile vanished, and her eyes darkened. "Here's the deal: I make your money problems go away—"

How can she know? "What money problems?"

"Come off it," she scoffed. "If you didn't owe some nasty people big-time, we wouldn't be talking. Right?"

Turner stared at her. "Go on."

"As I was saying, I get rid of your debt—right now—then you take out someone for me. And there'll be something extra for you once the job's done."

"What kind of bonus?"

She smiled. "It will be a surprise."

I should walk away. Turner frowned. *But I can't afford to.* "Who's the target?"

"We'll get to that *after* we've cleaned up your debt. That's your retainer." She paused. "But if you agree, there's no turning back. You follow through with the hit."

She leaned forward. "You don't want to have any enforcers coming around to collect on your $100,000 debt, do you?"

Turner swallowed hard. "How do you know—"

"About your debt? Remember, I'm connected." She pulled a thin notebook computer out of her tote bag. "I can make an electronic transfer immediately to whatever account you want. Deal?"

Turner hesitated. Accepting would be rolling the proverbial dice, and he was on a bad luck streak. But here was someone offering to pay off his marker. *Maybe my luck's about to change.*

"Deal." He pulled a pen and small notepad from his vest, scribbled, tore out a page and passed it to her. "Send the money there."

Sadie started to key in the transfer, paused and fixed her eyes on him. "Just so you know, if you run off or something happens to me, I've got 'insurance' to see you don't get far or live long. Got that?"

Is she bluffing? Turner thought of goons pursuing him and decided he couldn't take the chance. "Got it."

She finished typing and turned the laptop screen to face him. "Okay by you?"

Turner reviewed the data on the screen and nodded. She left the computer sitting on the table.

"Who's the target?"

Her reply was matter-of-fact. "Vito Volpone."

Turner groaned. His luck hadn't changed. He was still snakebit.

"Do you know what you're asking? I'm not prepared to take down a Mob boss." He swallowed the last of his beer. "It's a suicide mission. Volpone doesn't go around unprotected. And even if I pulled it off, his crew would be gunning for me. Count me out."

He started to rise, but Sadie clamped a hand on his forearm. "*Sit...down*," she hissed. "You'll do what I say, or you're a dead man."

He couldn't turn away from her icy blue gaze and lowered himself back into his seat.

He ran a hand over his graying buzz cut. "What's your beef with Volpone? Can't you work whatever it is out with him?"

She shook her head. "He doesn't forgive someone stealing from him."

Turner blinked in disbelief. "You?"

Sadie swallowed some beer. "Yes, but he thinks it was my husband. My *late* husband, Charlie Evans. He was an accountant for Volpone." She put down her drink, started typing and turned the computer screen toward Turner. "Check this."

CAR BLAST KILLS TWO, a headline trumpeted. Turner read the online report about the explosion in the driveway of a posh home and police finding the charred remains of two bodies, identified as Charles Evans and his wife Mercedes. "No suspects," he muttered. "Police are asking anyone with information…"

He finished reading and turned the screen back to Sadie. "It says Mrs. Evans was killed, so who are you?"

"I *am* Mercedes Evans. The woman in the car was a bimbo that Charlie planned to run off with once he'd helped himself to Volpone's cash." She gave a self-satisfied grin. "But I tipped off Volpone, and here we are."

Turner's mind was reeling. "What kind of bullshit is this?"

"No bullshit." She paused. "Let me back up a bit to help you understand."

He took a swig of beer. "I'm listenin'."

"Like I said, I was a military brat. I was five when my dad was killed. Mom remarried—another military man, she was comfortable with that lifestyle. Of course, we moved around. The last stop for me, before I finished high school, was a base in Arizona.

"I went on to college out east, graduated with an economics degree and landed a job with an accounting firm. That's where I met Charlie Evans.

"He was about nine years older than me and a star at the company." She closed her eyes and sighed. "God, he was handsome. About as tall as you, dark hair and eyes, athletic build. I was flattered that he was paying attention to me. The next thing you know, we're married and living the good life—fast cars, fancy clothes, posh home in an exclusive neighborhood. Foolish me, I thought I was set for life and left the firm.

"So one day, Charlie was running late for a meeting. He rushed out of the house and left his computer on. I was curious and started poking around in his files and emails. That's when I discovered he'd been cheating on me and that he was working for Volpone—not on all his accounts, but the ones Charlie handled and could access added up to a healthy seven figures."

"So you were mad at him for running around," Turner interrupted. "Why not ask for a divorce?"

"Because Charlie could afford a lawyer who would see that I didn't get a cent." Sadie glared at him. "I wasn't going to leave empty-handed."

She paused and asked, "Shall I proceed?"

Turner nodded.

"I didn't say anything about what I'd found. Instead, I waited to learn more," she continued. "I couldn't count on Charlie to always be careless, so I found a hacker to get me into his computers—home and office—and smartphone. While he was at it, he got me into Volpone's as well. Passwords, emails, texts, files and bank accounts were all at my fingertips. When I had what I needed, I confronted Charlie about the affair. I stormed out, saying I was going to stay with my mother—I didn't—and that he'd hear from my lawyer. Chrissie—a redhead I'd seen around the office—moved into the house, while I—unbeknownst to them—got an apartment under my maiden name.

"I kept an eye on Charlie's emails and texts. When I saw that Chrissie was pushing him to run off with Volpone's money, I put together what you'd call an improvised explosive device—"

Turner's eye widened. "*You* planted the car bomb?"

"Hey, why look so surprised?" Sadie replied. "There's plenty of how-to information on the Internet. And I picked up a lot living on military bases.

"When the blast went off, I moved Volpone's money into an account I had set up for myself. Then I called him. 'It's Mercedes Evans, Charlie's wife. He's going to run off with your money.' I whispered, pretended I was frightened.

'It wasn't my idea. I don't want to get in trouble with you. He's coming. Gotta go,' I said to him. Then I hung up."

"Unbelievable." Turner shook his head. "Volpone thinks you and Charlie were both killed in the blast, and so do the police. Seems to me like you're in the clear."

"For now," Sadie answered. "Right now, the cops see this as a Mob hit, but don't know whether Volpone or The Chicken Man is behind it."

Turner nodded at the Chicken Man reference. The rival bosses of the city's underworld, Vito "The Fox" Volpone and Gino "The Chicken Man" Ciccone had fallen into an unspoken truce that allowed their criminal enterprises to flourish.

"Volpone's fuming, but he's too smart to go to war with Ciccone without hard proof," Sadie said. "But at some point, the cops will figure out it wasn't me in the car. They'll be looking for me, then so will Volpone." She paused. "Unless he's gone."

Sadie swallowed the last of her beer. "The way I figure it, once Volpone's dead, there will be a power struggle inside his gang, Ciccone will try to move in and the cops will have their hands full with a Mob war. That's when I'll disappear."

"Why me?"

"I came across your name—and your IOU—in one of Charlie's files. I knew I'd need help, and I figured your military experience—yes, I looked that up—would be an asset."

Suddenly, she cocked her head at the strains of a new track on the jukebox—Creedence Clearwater Revival's "Run Through the Jungle." "I just *love* CCR, don't you?"

Turner winced. "They were good, but that song..." He shook his head. He wasn't about to tell her that it brought back memories of a mission gone terribly wrong. "Never mind. You were saying?"

She smiled. "So I decided to buy your services. And as I told you, I have 'insurance,' so don't cross me."

Turner leaned back in his seat. *I better play along—for now.* "What's the plan?"

"First, we fly to Arizona."

"Huh?"

She pointed at his tattoo. "To see some of those."

***

"We'll be there soon," Sadie said as she guided a rental Jeep around a rut in a dirt road in southeast Arizona.

Turner snuck an admiring look at her legs.

"See something you like?" Sadie grinned. "Is that sunburn or a blush?"

Damn! "Just drive," he grumbled as he looked out at the desert terrain.

She gave a mock salute. "Yes, sir!"

He turned back to her. "I've been meaning to ask you since the airport, what's with your shirt?" Her red T-shirt featured a woman's face—blank eyes like on a Greek statue, full lips, straight-edged nose—topped with and framed by snakes instead of hair.

She glanced at him, then back to the road. "Medusa."

"Yeah. Anyone who looked at her turned to stone, right?"

"Right. She stopped them dead in their tracks, you might say." She laughed.

"You tryin' to make some kind of statement?"

"No, I just like the design. I thought I should wear something to go with your tattoo."

They drove in silence for a few minutes before Turner said, "You still haven't told me why we're here." He looked around. "Wherever *here* is."

"The base is over that way." She pointed her chin to the right. "But we're headed for Rancho Rodriguez. About five more minutes."

She said nothing more until they stopped at a driveway with an overhead sign announcing they'd arrived at Rancho Rodriguez. She proceeded down the drive and pulled up in front of a ranch-style bungalow with a screened-in veranda and an attached garage. A backhoe loader was parked beside it. A little to his right, Turner saw a gray cinder-block building with a small porch.

The front door of the house opened, and out stepped a Hispanic man—muscular, black hair, pencil mustache. He was about her height—five foot nine, he guessed. She hopped down from the Jeep and ran to embrace him.

"Meet Mateo Rodriguez." She motioned Turner to come over. "Best snake wrangler in Arizona."

Rodriguez grinned and squeezed Turner's hand. "Pleased to meet you, *señor.*"

Turner flinched and turned away from the small dark eyes in Rodriguez's weather-creased face that were boring into him.

Then Rodriguez fixed his gaze on Turner's snake tattoo. "*El serpiente de cascabel.* You like?" He laughed. "You have come to the right place."

Turner flexed his fingers as Rodriquez released his grip.

Rodriguez turned to the cinder-block building and motioned to Turner and Sadie to follow him. "Come! I have some work to do. Sadie, she has seen this many times, but you will find it interesting, *señor.*"

"How did you meet this guy?" Turner asked Sadie as they followed him.

"I used to ride horses out here when I was a teenager," Sadie replied. "One day, my horse got spooked by a rattler. I was thrown, but luckily for me, Mateo was in the area hunting for snakes. He captured the rattler, calmed my horse and got me back to the base. The medic told me I was lucky I hadn't been bitten and only had a few scrapes and bruises.

"I looked Mateo up to thank him. He showed me around his place and explained what he did. I became fascinated with his snakes and his work, and offered to help him in any way I could."

"This is a *business*?"

"Quite profitable, actually." She paused. "I guess you could say Mateo became my mentor. I learned about snakes and the desert. We kept in touch after I went to college— and after I married Charlie."

Rodriguez stopped in front of the cinder-block building. "*Mi casa de serpientes*. Wait here, *por favor.*"

"That's Mateo's snake house," she said. "He's got about a dozen or more species in there, mainly rattlers, a couple of hundred snakes altogether. The interior is light- and temperature-controlled."

Rodriguez emerged from the snake house with a few clear plastic bins, each holding a rattlesnake, and long-handled metal tongs with a C-shaped end.

"What's he going to do?" Turner asked.

"Milk them." Sadie laughed at Turner's puzzled look. "Extract their venom."

Using the tongs, Rodriguez lifted a snake about three and a half feet long from one of the bins. The rattler had brown blotches that stretched down its back and faded into white and black bands at its tail.

"That's a Mojave rattler," she said. "It has the most potent rattlesnake venom." She paused. "There are two strains of Mojave rattler venom. One strain, considered the more lethal, attacks the nervous system; the other destroys red blood cells. Some Mojaves have strains of both."

"How do you know this?"

"A bit of research. I've learned to respect all rattlers. It's best to stay out of their way."

Rodriguez placed the snake on a foam pad on a small table. At the table's edge was a glass funnel—its mouth covered by a thin, waxy membrane—suspended over a vial.

He grabbed the snake with his left hand and fit the snake's fangs over the side of the funnel. The rattler bit the membrane, releasing a yellowish venom. With his thumb and middle finger, he depressed two glands near the reptile's jaw to extract all the venom. Then he maneuvered the snake back into its bin.

Rodriguez repeated the procedure with more snakes that hissed and rattled to signal their displeasure, until the vial was about three-quarters full.

"All that trouble for *that*?" Turner remarked.

"*Oro, señor*," Rodriguez replied as he capped the vial.

"Liquid gold," Sadie said. "It's worth thousands. He freeze–dries it and ships it to clinics, labs and universities. They use it for research and to make antivenom."

Rodriguez beckoned them to follow him into the snake house. "Come! Let me show you my beauties." He ushered them in and stopped to place the vial in a compact fridge. Then he pointed to racks that ran the length of the building along two walls, and beamed. "There are Mojaves, western diamondbacks, sidewinders, corals—"

"That's it for me." The snake house was creeping Turner out. "I'll wait outside."

Rodriguez shook his head in feigned disappointment and pointed at Turner's tattoo. "*Señor*, I thought you might enjoy being among your own kind."

He laughed as Turner glared at him. "Forgive my little joke, *por favor.*" He clapped his hands. "Come! Let us go into *mi casa* for some *cervezas.*"

***

"There, *chiquita.*" Rodriguez placed a small square metal case on his living room table and a longer metal case beside his armchair. He opened the small case and turned it to face Sadie and Turner, who were seated across from him on a leather couch.

"Your special order," Rodriguez said.

Inside the foam-lined case were what Turner recognized as tranquilizer darts that held a yellowish substance.

"I thought we were going after Volpone, not putting critters to sleep," Turner said. Then he realized Rodriguez was watching and listening. *Shit! Have I said too much?* He turned to Sadie. "Does he know about—?"

"*Si, señor,*" Rodriguez interjected. "Sadie has told me her plan."

"Are you going to fill *me* in?" Turner asked.

Sadie turned to face him. "We're going to take Volpone down with these." She pointed to the darts.

Turner looked at them. "Is that yellow stuff what I think it is?"

Sadie nodded. "Mojave venom, what Mateo was milking." She turned to Rodriguez. "Can we see the rifle, Mateo?"

Rodriguez moved the dart case from the table, brought out the longer case and opened it. At first glance, Turner thought he was looking at a hunting rifle. Then he recognized the components of an air gun—long barrel, telescopic sight, wooden stock, compressed carbon dioxide cartridges.

Turner inspected the pieces and returned them to the case. "What kind of range does it have?"

"More than enough to give you cover and hit Volpone," Sadie replied. "That's why I brought you in. You're a marksman, I'm not. Who better to administer a lethal dose of venom than The Snake?" She laughed.

Turner shifted uncomfortably in his seat. "Why all this poison dart bullshit? Why not a bullet to the head? Bam! It's over."

"Because I don't *want* it to be over like *that!*" Sadie said with a snarl as she snapped her fingers. "Volpone's made a lot of people suffer, so I want *him* to suffer, to *know* something's wrong, maybe realize he's *dying*."

This is insane! Gotta talk her out of this. "I heard that not many snakebites are fatal."

"Only if they're treated quickly," Sadie said. "Even if his goons get Volpone to a hospital in short order—which they won't—they won't be able to tell doctors what's in his system, and the doctors won't have time to figure it out."

"So what happens to Volpone once he's hit?"

"Let's see." She counted off on her fingers as she recited. "Shortness of breath, double vision, difficulty swallowing and speaking, nausea, weakness or paralysis of the lower limbs, involuntary tremors of facial muscles and respiratory failure."

She turned to Rodriguez. "That about cover it?"

"*Si, chiquita.*" Rodriguez smiled as he regarded Turner. "This man who is bitten, he will soon be one of *los muertos.*"

"With a dart, how long before he's dead?" Turner asked.

"It's not instant, like in the movies. Maybe 10 minutes, maybe hours." Sadie shrugged. "It doesn't matter."

She stood and pulled her notebook computer out of her shoulder bag. "Take care of this for me, will you, Mateo?"

"Of course, *chiquita*." Rodriguez took the laptop from her.

Sadie faced Turner. "I access my money from that. There's a sealed envelope with the password in a safe deposit box, and Mateo has the key. So it's in your best interest that we both return."

Turner cursed silently. *So that's her 'insurance.' I'm stuck with the job.*

"*Sólo un momento.*" Rodriguez hurried out of the room and returned with a black smartphone case with a small cartridge clipped to one side. "For you, *chiquita*."

Sadie turned the case over in her hand as she examined it, then slipped her phone into it. "*Gracias, Mateo.*"

"*De nada.*"

"What's that for?" Turner asked.

"Extra protection. The cartridge holds pepper spray. It has a range of 10 feet." She attached the phone to her shorts and tugged her T-shirt over it. "We better get going."

Pepper spray. Poison darts. I've gotta be careful around her. But once I have my bonus, she's history.

Turner picked up the cases. "Where to now?"

"Feelin' lucky? Volpone's off to Vegas and so are we."

* * *

Sadie stepped out of the Jeep and spun around to face Turner. "How do I look?" She was dressed in black capris and flats and a long-sleeved white shirt. Her blond hair was tucked under a black bob-with-bangs wig.

He grinned. "Like that broad in *Pulp Fiction*."

It was two days later, and they were parked beside a mountain lodge—a large A-frame log house with a wraparound deck, about an hour's drive from Las Vegas and accessible only by a dirt road that wound its way up through pines and aspens.

Turner's smile quickly faded. "I still don't like it. What if Volpone recognizes you?"

"Why should he? We've only met a few times when I was with Charlie, and even then only briefly. I doubt he'd remember my voice. When I called him after I killed Charlie, I was all frantic whispers."

Sadie patted her wig. "Besides, I'm no longer a blonde, and I'm supposed to be dead."

"I still can't picture Volpone coming here."

She sighed in exasperation. "I already *told* you. Volpone sees himself as a hunter, and there's plenty of game around here—bighorn sheep, deer, mountain lions. Every year, he takes his family to Vegas. They stay on The Strip for the shows, he comes up here with a couple of his boys—usually just the driver and a bodyguard—to hunt. He rents different spots, but there's always someone from the rental agency to meet him and hand over the keys.

"From my email and text surveillance, I found out when he was arriving. I phoned the agency, pretended to represent Volpone and told them he'd be a day late, but to hold his cabin reservation. No problem, they assured me." She paused. "But Volpone is coming today. I'm the agency rep with the keys."

"Don't tell me you *really* have the keys."

She laughed. "Of course not." She paused. "Now go over what you have to do."

Turner pointed to a copse of pines about 20 yards away. "I'll be over there, loaded and waiting. Once Volpone and his men move away from their car, I dart one guard.

He goes down, I dart the other. You pepper-spray Volpone, then I dart him."

"That's it." She looked at her watch. "You better set up. They should be here in about half an hour."

As he headed for the trees with the rifle and dart cases, he thought of his own "insurance"—a Glock in an ankle holster strapped to his right leg, hidden beneath his jeans. He had filled out the paperwork allowing him to stow the gun in a locked case as part of his checked luggage on the Arizona flight. He'd declared it, as required, to the airline, but he hadn't told Sadie.

***

Turner stood between a pair of trees, far enough away from the lodge that he wouldn't be spotted. As a black Lincoln Town Car pulled up in front of the lodge, he pressed the rifle's stock against his right shoulder and lined up its scope. Two men emerged on the passenger side of the vehicle and one on the driver's side. Sadie, who'd been checking her smartphone on the deck, tucked it into her shoulder bag and stepped out to greet them.

There was no mistaking Volpone—six feet tall, lean, slicked-back gray hair, aquiline nose and jutting chin. His two "soldiers" were slightly shorter than him, broad-shouldered and muscular. They wore standard hunting attire—plaid flannel shirts, jeans, boots—except for the Smith & Wesson handguns in shoulder holsters.

Turner followed them with the scope as they moved toward Sadie. *That's it. Away from the car.*

They took a few more steps before Volpone held up his hand. He and his men stopped. So did Sadie.

"Who are you?" Volpone demanded. "Where's Dave? The agency always sends Dave."

"I'm Mia. Dave called in sick today, but he should be here tomorrow to see that you have everything you need. I'm here to let you in and give you the keys."

Volpone hesitated. "You look kind of familiar."

Sadie laughed. "I get that all the time. People say I look like Uma Thurman in *Pulp Fiction*." She started to fumble in her tote bag. "Now where are those keys?" Volpone's men moved to grab their guns.

"Relax, fellas. Why so jumpy? It's just my phone." She eased it out of the bag and held it up. "See?" The mobsters lowered their hands from their holsters.

"Okay, boys. Go get our gear." Volpone turned to Sadie. "Let's see those keys."

My cue. The rifle gave a soft *pop* as Turner fired. The dart hit one of the men in the thigh, prompting him to look down. "What the fuck?" he cried as he crumpled to the ground.

Pop! Turner hit second man below the knee, and he collapsed.

Before Volpone could turn to see what was happening, Sadie blasted him with pepper spray.

"Argh!" Volpone threw his hands up to his eyes, coughed and staggered backward. Sadie reached into his holster, grabbed his gun and flung it behind her.

Pop! Turner sent a dart into Volpone's shoulder.

Volpone's guards struggled to reach for their guns but failed. Sadie sprayed their faces and tossed their weapons aside. Then she stepped back and sat on the edge of the deck.

Turner loaded another dart into the rifle, aimed at Volpone again, then swung the weapon around to put Sadie in the crosshairs. *It would be so easy to do it!* He hesitated. *I can't.* He fired a dart into Volpone's thigh. *I need to collect my bonus first.*

He stepped out from behind the trees and sat down beside her. "Now what?"

"We collect the guns and darts, then head back to Mateo's. But for now—" she pointed her chin at the mobsters "—we wait for them to die."

They sat in silence as Volpone and his men coughed, gasped and moaned before they stopped breathing.

***

Turner shuddered as CCR's "Bad Moon Rising" came over the Jeep's speakers. John Fogerty was warning about trouble on the way. He shook his head. *Get a grip. It's just a song.*

"Something wrong?" Sadie asked. "Want me to change the station?" She'd gone back to wearing the Medusa T-shirt and denim shorts.

"Leave it on and keep goin'." He thought of the Glock strapped to his ankle. *Bang! Bang! No more Rodriguez, no more Sadie.*

Half an hour later, they pulled into Rancho Rodriguez. It was nearly dark, but there were no lights on inside the bungalow.

"Mateo!" Sadie called out as she stepped from the Jeep. "We're here." There was no answer. "Mateo!"

Turner stayed in his seat and turned toward the snake house. A short distance away, he saw the backhoe, mounds of dirt and a shovel.

He eased the Glock out of its ankle holster, then turned, pointing the gun at Sadie and motioning her to get back into the Jeep. "Keep your hands where I can see 'em."

She slowly opened the driver's door, raised her hands and slid into the seat.

"*Señor*, over here!"

The voice came from somewhere behind him, near the corner of the house. As he turned his head to see where

Rodriguez was, he felt Sadie's hand slam into his neck. He cried out. She grabbed his gun hand and struck it against the dashboard; the gun fell to the Jeep floor.

Pain shot up Turner's arm and around his neck. As he struggled to get his bearings, Sadie retrieved the Glock. He twisted in his seat to see Rodriguez advancing with a shotgun. He looked back at Sadie and saw her swing the gun at his head.

Then everything went black.

***

When he came to, Turner was lying face up, his hands taped in front of him. He swiveled his head to either side and saw walls of dirt about four feet high.

A pit. His eyes widened. "Help!"

He tried to move his feet, but they were also bound. His head and his arm throbbed. He looked up to see a full moon in the night sky.

He positioned his knees as if he were going to do sit-ups. Bending at the waist, he rocked forward, struggling to sit up. The effort left him panting.

Sadie loomed over him. "If you're thinking of yelling for help, save your breath. No one will hear you. It's just you, me, Mateo and the snakes."

Dread washed over Turner. "I did what you wanted." He bowed his head on his knees. "Volpone's dead. Forget about the bonus. Just let me go."

"Sorry, Turner. I have a score to settle."

"I don't understand."

"Maybe this will help." She placed a portable Bluetooth speaker at the edge of the pit, pulled an iPod from her shorts pocket and poised her index finger over its face. "This one's for you."

Then Turner heard the opening sound effects of CCR's "Run Through the Jungle."

"Before I was Mercedes Evans, I was Mercedes Hunter," Sadie said as John Fogerty started to sing. "I'm Nate Hunter's daughter. Remember him?"

Turner collapsed on his back and shut his eyes. *Hunter!*

***

The memories that Turner had tried to block out for years washed over him as he lay in the pit.

It was 1994, about two months before Operation Uphold Democracy, intended to remove Haiti's military regime. His Delta Force unit—himself, Michael Doyle, Nate Hunter, Eric Grant, Reed Matthews, Mark Brady—had been assigned to destroy a barracks and ammunition depot in the northwest.

The plan called for a quick strike: land in a rigid inflatable boat on a beach about half a mile from the target compound, located farther down the beach; conceal the Zodiac and edge through the jungle skirting the beach; under cover of darkness, plant plastic explosives and timers; begin to sneak back to the hidden boat; set off the explosives; head out to sea to be picked up by a Coast Guard cutter.

The plan had gone smoothly—the beach landing, cutting through the razor wire, planting explosives—until he checked his watch. That's when he heard the chatter of automatic gunfire. One of his men had been spotted.

"Hunter!" He turned to the operator who'd been working with him. "Everything set?"

"Ready to go off like the Fourth of July."

"Then let's get the hell out of here."

Turner dashed for the opening in the razor wire, with Hunter close behind. He and Hunter waved through Doyle and Grant. "Get to the boat! Hunter, you go with 'em!"

He turned back to face the compound and got his MP5 submachine gun ready.

His last two men, Matthews and Brady, scrambled through the opening in the razor wire. Matthews had his right arm slung over Brady's shoulders; he'd been hit in the right leg.

Gunfire sounded behind them. "Move it! Move it!" he urged as they limped along the beach toward the jungle.

Suddenly a series of blasts shook the ground beneath him. Turner saw fires light up the night sky above the compound. "Yes!" he cried, raising a fist.

Then he spotted Matthews and Brady sprawled in the sand, unmoving, a few feet away. *Nothing I can do for them. Have to save myself.* He started running for the boat.

Crashing through the jungle, he heard yells and sporadic gunfire behind him. He quickened his pace to take advantage of the Haitians' confusion.

As he neared the rendezvous, he heard more gunfire just ahead of him. The shooting stopped seconds before he stumbled out of the jungle.

In the moonlight, he could see their boat at the edge of the water and six bodies, four of whom he didn't recognize. He quickly assessed what had happened: A Haitian patrol had surprised his men as they were dragging the boat toward the water. Everyone had opened fire; Hunter, Grant and four Haitians had gone down. Where was Doyle?

"Don't shoot!" Doyle stepped out from behind some foliage. "Hunter thought he heard something and sent me out to take a look. I cut through the jungle and heard shots. That patrol must have come up the beach. I hurried back but..." He peered into the darkness behind Turner. "Brady? Matthews?"

"Dead." Turner shook his head. "We gotta move. Get the boat into the water!"

As they got the boat into the water, they heard a groan from one of the bloodied bodies.

"H-help me," Hunter's feeble voice croaked.

Doyle started to move toward Hunter. Turner grabbed his arm, but Doyle twisted free. "We can't leave Hunter," Doyle insisted. "It's not right."

"Hear that?" Sounds of yells and gunfire drew nearer. "We don't have time. Leave him."

"We can't!"

"I'm in charge, and I say we can!" Turner fired at the bodies of Hunter and Grant. Blood mingled with the seawater. "You wanna join 'em?" He pointed his gun at Doyle. "Choose."

Doyle glared at Turner in disgust, but pushed the boat into the water.

They said nothing until they neared the pickup vessel.

"Leave the talking to me," Turner said. "The target was hit, then everything went to hell. We lost some good men, but were lucky to get out. End of story. My word against yours, so let's be on the same page. Okay?"

Doyle stared at him for a moment. "This'll come back to bite you."

"Not if you go along. Your ass is in the sling as much as mine."

Doyle cast down his eyes and nodded.

***

The higher-ups bought the story. He left the force, Doyle stayed. Case closed.

But since then, everything in Turner's life had come up snake eyes.

Guns and explosives were his stock-in-trade, so he joined a private military company. But he balked at being a contractor in global hot spots. He drifted into the underworld, serving as muscle and a gun for hire for the Mob.

Working for the Mob did not provide a windfall, so he tried to change his fortunes at the gambling tables. He enjoyed a modest winning streak, but greed got the better of him. Instead of cashing in, he'd ended up in the hole to Volpone.

Then Sadie walked into The Hideaway, and now he was in a far deeper hole.

***

"Run Through the Jungle" faded into the desert night. It was cool, but Turner broke into a sweat. *How much does she know?* He decided that pleading ignorance would be his best strategy. He looked up at Sadie. "N-Nate who?"

"Come off it." Her voice was filled with disdain. "My father was part of a raid on Haiti in '94. You led the unit. Six men went in, only two came out."

Turner swallowed hard. "You've got it all wrong."

"No, I haven't," Sadie snapped. "My mother and I heard it all from Michael Doyle."

I should have shot him when I had the chance. "Whatever he told you was a lie."

"I don't see why a dying man would lie." She paused. "We were living on the base down here, 10 years after my father was killed. Doyle looked us up, he was dying of cancer. He wanted to atone for his sins, as he put it, and he figured we were owed the truth. He regretted not helping Dad, was ashamed of not saying what really happened that night. He told us how you killed him." She pointed to Turner's tattoo. "And how we could pick you out."

"I didn't do anything."

"*Liar!*" she screamed. She took a moment to compose herself. "Okay, let's continue. My stepfather's okay, but Mom lost her soul mate and I grew up without my real dad. We wanted justice."

She ran a hand through her hair. "Doyle told us you'd quit after the raid and he didn't know where you were. Personnel records went as far as your discharge. That was the end of it for Mom. But I promised myself if I ever found you, I'd make you pay. How I'd find you, I had no idea." She paused. "Things just...*happened*. First Charlie, then Volpone, then you."

Turner struggled back into a sit-up position. "So finding me was pure chance."

"I prefer to think of it as destiny."

"Bullshit! Like that so-called bonus."

"Mateo!" she called over her shoulder, then looked back at Turner. "Bonus? Your word, not mine. I said there'd be *something extra* for you. This is it."

Turner bowed his head. "No, no..."

"*Buenas noches, señor.*" Rodriguez was standing next to Sadie, holding a pair of snake tongs dangling a rattler. "A Mojave for you." He dropped the snake into a corner of the pit.

Turner pushed himself up against a dirt wall across from the snake. The Mojave hissed, coiled up and rattled its tail. As he stared at it wide-eyed, another one landed in his lap and slithered down his thigh.

"Better not move, Turner," Sadie said. "You don't want to get them more agitated."

A third snake landed on his shoulders, while a fourth came down at his feet.

"What happened to that code of no one left behind?" she said. "Four men abandoned, four snakes for you. Poetic justice, I'd say."

"P-please!" Turner begged. "G-get me out of here!"

"Like you got my father out of Haiti?" Sadie sneered. "You *murdered* him!"

"No, it wasn't—" He looked down and screamed as a snake sank its fangs into his thigh. He felt another set of fangs bite into his neck.

He felt nauseous. He looked up to see Sadie scoop a shovelful of earth and throw it down onto his lap. The snakes became agitated, slithered around his arms and legs, and bit again.

"From dust to dust." She threw more dirt on him before putting the shovel down and wiping her hands. "Better get the backhoe going, Mateo." She looked down at Turner. "Makes it so much easier to dig and fill in a grave."

Turner tried to speak, but managed only a strangled groan.

Sadie waggled the fingers of her right hand. "Bye, Turner." Then she disappeared.

Turner struggled to breathe; his legs stiffened. *It can't end like this! It can't!* A vision of the Medusa on Sadie's T-shirt floated before his eyes. He realized that, like the Gorgon's victims, he'd soon be stone-cold dead.

The last sounds he heard were the buzz from the rattlers and the rumble of the backhoe.

About Ed Piwowarczyk

Ed Piwowarczyk is a veteran journalist, having worked as a copy editor for the *National Post* and *Toronto Sun*, and as an editor and reporter for the *Sault Star*. As well, he has edited Harlequin novels on a freelance basis, and is currently a freelance editor.

A lifelong fan of crime fiction, he is also a film buff and plays in the Canadian Inquisition, a Toronto pub trivia league. His short fiction has appeared in *World Enough and Crime*, *13 O'Clock* and *The Whole She-Bang 3*.

AFTERWORD
By M.H. Callway

On behalf of the Mesdames of Mayhem, I would like to thank Donna Carrick and Carrick Publishing for their wonderful support in bringing our readers three collections of crime stories: *Thirteen*, *13 O'Clock*, and now *13 Claws*.

The Mesdames are committed to promoting Canadian crime writing. Many of us teach creative writing and mentor emerging writers, so for *13 Claws* we held a contest for authors who had never before published a crime fiction story.

We are delighted to present the winning story, "Night Vision" by Mary Patterson, and the two runners-up, "Dana's Cat" by Rosalind Place and "That Damn Cat" by Marilyn Kay.

We hope to read more of their crime fiction in the future.

M.H. Callway
Founder, The Mesdames of Mayhem

We hope you have enjoyed our quirky crime anthology.

We're thrilled to share with you our love of animals and our passion for a good story.

If our tales left you feeling connected with our authors, don't hesitate to reach out to each of them at the links we've provided in their profiles.

Wishing you joyous reading!

Donna Carrick
Carrick Publishing

76336087R00156

Made in the USA
Columbia, SC
05 September 2017